THE SYRIAN PEDDLER

Dear Jerry,

Enjoy!

Uncle

Lol.

Lloyd

THE SYRIAN PEDDLER

Linda Hanna Lloyd

Cover Photography by Wilbur McIntosh,
McIntosh Photography, Brownsville, PA

ISBN: 9781793242518

Independently Published via KDP

For my father, Louis F. Hanna who always had a good story to tell.

PREFACE

This book is a labor of love—and the story of my Syrian grandparents. My memories of my grandfather, *Gidu* and my grandmother, *Situ*, go back to my kindergarten days in Masontown, Pennsylvania. I still have vivid pictures in my mind of Hanna's Department Store and their home, including the basement, garage, and back alley. Sam and Anna Hanna were an attractive couple. I remember him as being a very kind, gentle man. I remember her as always being in the kitchen or else welcoming customers into the store. *Gidu* and *Situ* spoke English as well as Arabic in their home. They loved to entertain family and friends with amazing Syrian dishes.

I was just starting first grade when my parents moved from Masontown. Dad would take me back to visit as often as possible—it was a six-hour drive. I would play with my cousins, and we would spend the night. Dad would buy what we needed from the store.

Gidu lived several years past *Situ*'s death. I clearly remember the night my father received the call that *Gidu* had had a heart attack. He didn't die immediately, so Dad had time to say goodbye. I was sixteen at the time. Later, I regretted never having asked *Gidu* about his and *Situ*'s immigration, their early days, and their eventual move from New Salem to Masontown. As an adult, however, I became interested in my heritage, and I began to ask relatives for details and to investigate my family history. Everything I learned became a part of this fictionalized account of Sam and Anna Hanna and their family.

PART I

Saddo Ibn Hanna

"Do what you can, with what you have, where you are."

THEODORE ROOSEVELT

1

After a few nights on board, he was bored. *What is there to do but walk around the upper deck, talk to people, and write in my journal?*

At breakfast on the third morning, Saddo heard that the chef needed help in the ship's kitchen. He quickly finished a bowl of porridge, went back to his cabin, and sat on the edge of the bed, running his hands through his hair and surveying the room. His darbuka was on the floor. Lying at the foot of the bed were his journal, his Bible, and a book. Other than those four objects, his only possessions at this moment were three changes of clothes and a second pair of boots. Hidden in those boots and wrapped in socks were his liras.

Suddenly, he jumped up, darted out the door, and headed toward the kitchen quarters. "Hello, sir," he told the man who appeared to be in charge. "Is it true that you're looking for kitchen help? If so, I'm interested."

"Yes, that's true. I'm Chef Juan Severino."

"Saddo Hanna. Pleased to meet you, Mr. Severino."

The man narrowed his eyes while shaking the hand Saddo had offered him. "So tell me about yourself—and why you want to work."

Saddo launched into the speech he'd prepared. "I just left my home in Damascus, Syria, where I completed my schooling while working in the family business. Why do I want to work for you? Well, I like to keep my hands and mind busy. And I could use the earnings to repay my father for my first-class ticket."

By now, Juan Severino's face had relaxed a bit. "We generally don't hire passengers. But luck may be with you. One of my staff became ill before we left port. . . . A first-class passenger working in my kitchen." He smirked. "And what does your father do?"

"He has a successful export business dealing with merchants from many countries. I'm going to America to work with one of my father's apprentices."

"Then he does very well—and that explains your first-class ticket. You appear to be a capable young man to help with dinner preparations. And since you speak English, you can assist Giuseppe serving in the first-class dining room. Also, at times I may ask you to help in steerage. We have eighteen first-class passengers and about a thousand in steerage." He paused. "I warn you, though, many passengers will soon be sick as dogs, and even the idea of food will be repugnant. Then the dining room becomes a challenge." The man looked Saddo up and down. "Yes, you'll do. Check with me in the morning for your daily schedule."

Saddo shook hands with the chef once more. "Thank you, sir. I'll see you in the morning."

Back in his cabin, Saddo absentmindedly flipped through his journal. Then he picked up the only book he'd brought with him—Ada Goodrich-Freer's *In a Syrian Saddle*— and began to read. But the woman's writing couldn't hold his interest either. His mind wandered back to the rich environment, full of beautiful objects, that he'd left behind, and he compared that to his present surroundings. Suddenly he remembered one other object in his possession: a tiny replica of the magnificent Greek Orthodox Church his family attended. His eyes brightened as he pulled it out of a boot and carefully removed it from a sock. After turning it round and round, he placed it on the small shelf by the bed and began to write in his journal.

"Am I late?" She lifted a corner of her skirt to keep from tripping. Her petticoat peeked out from under her dress, which was the color of summer grass.

As she picked up a plate at the serving table, it slipped to the floor. Saddo wasted no time in picking up the shards for her.

Standing again, with the pieces in his hand, he gazed in wonder at the slim young woman before him. *How different from the girls at home.* Her auburn hair reminded him of the copper jewelry his uncle designed. Even though her cheeks were red as cherries at that moment, her skin was as light

When she brushed away a tear, Saddo noticed her eyes—the color of the turquoise bead his mother wore on a gold chain. He said, "Hello. My name is Saddo Hanna. Don't worry."

"Thank you." She said this shyly, regaining her composure, and daintily turned to sit down for dinner. He watched her as she talked to the couple across the table.

That evening, after his work shift, Saddo was on the upper deck, lightly drumming his darbuka Only a few days into the crossing, the children had already come to love sitting at his feet and watching him. Tonight three young boys accompanied him, clapping their hands to the beat of his drum.

When he finished playing, he looked up. *There she is—looking sad. Like my mother when she hugged me goodbye.* Saddo walked quickly toward her, as if she might disappear any second.

She tried to smile, her perky nose sprinkled with a few freckles. "Hello, Saddo. Forgive me for being in such a rush at dinner. I dropped that plate and didn't thank you for helping me. Or even tell you my name. I'm Emma Monahan." Now she grinned. "I have to be more careful or else I'll be buying new plates for the ship."

Saddo laughed. "You won't have to buy plates." He nervously twirled the darbuka around. His next words came out so much faster and louder than usual that he didn't recognize himself. "I noticed your accent. You're Irish, maybe? Where are you going to live in America?"

Emma seemed surprised by his interest. She moved away from the railing as she fussed with her skirt. "Yes, I'm from Ireland, traveling to New York City to live with my cousin, Bernadette. We grew up together in Limerick. Our fathers own the Cruises Royal Hotel there. By chance, the man and woman sitting across from me at dinner are from Limerick too." She caught her breath. "And you?"

"I'm from Damascus, Syria. My family traveled to Beirut, in Lebanon, with me. In Beirut I boarded a small steamer that transports passengers to Marseilles. There were only about a hundred of us on that boat."

"If I may ask, why are you working during the crossing?"

"The money will go toward fulfilling my dream. To own a business." He shrugged. "Besides, there's not much else to do." Then he finished his short list of reasons with a smile. "Furthermore, I met *you*."

"You did. And what a way to meet me." She sounded amused and jittery at the same time. "I really was in a hurry. But then I always seem to be. After school—I was in the upper level at St. Mary's Catholic—I rushed to my piano lessons, and then it was off to the hotel to study or help my parents."

Emma paused for another breath. "You're ambitious to find work on the ship."

At these words, he smoothed his shirt collar and tried not to look too proud. "I like hard work. After school and on weekends, I helped my father at his business."

"What kind of business?"

"He works with other merchants to export goods—mainly silks. He taught me the art and the science of marketing—but also honesty and fairness."

"Silk fabric, or clothing made of silk?"

"Mostly fabric. But also robes, jackets, pillows. I can still picture my mother in her silk jacket the morning I set sail from Beirut. It was a deep blue, with mauve embroidered squares and circles down the front."

"It sounds beautiful. In my country, jackets trimmed in lace are popular with the women. My mother taught me to design and sew lace collars."

"I'd like to see your lace if you have any with you."

"I'll show you. But another time, of course. Right now it's time for me to return to my cabin."

"Before you go, will you walk around the deck with me?" Emma hesitated. "Yes, but not for long."

Saddo wanted to take her hand—but that would be unheard of. And he sensed that Emma was keeping their bodies from coming too close together. *All the girls I know are Syrian. What is it about Emma? Her accent, fair skin, dots of freckles, all are very different. Yet looking at her makes my head feel fuzzy.*

He stopped at the entrance of a passageway and opened a door. The steps, made of wooden slats, led to the kitchen. It surprised him how quickly they had become so familiar.

Emma moved in toward Saddo. Her voice slightly trembling, she said, "Where do these steps go? I confess I'm a bit frightened. And I don't want to cause trouble. Are we allowed here?"

"Yes, we can be here. This leads to the storage area for the kitchen. The other workers and I come up these steps during the daytime for fresh air. Trust me. No one in the crew will mind if we sit on these steps and talk after the evening meal. *Rajaa'an.* Meet me here tomorrow evening after dinner." The Arabic word had slipped from his mouth.

"What did you say? Rahaa . . .?"

"It means 'please.'"

THE SYRIAN PEDDLER

The next morning Saddo was wakened by the steamer's slow but violent movements, from up to down, from starboard to port. He went to the deck and watched the high, dark waves rushing toward the vessel as if they wanted to jump on board. *It's not going to be a good day in the kitchen.* He wondered how Emma was.

Chef Juan met with his staff. "The seas are to be rough all day," he announced. "For breakfast, serve the porridge. For lunch and dinner, prepare bland soups. Slice potatoes and carrots thin and add a mild broth. Make sure the tea is hot. We'll do our best. The captain and the crew will want to make sure that soup is ready for anyone who calls for food during the night."

As they sliced and diced, the five men in the kitchen traded stories. They were an interesting blend: two Italians named Giuseppe and Mario, André from France, and Diego, who was Spanish. Saddo was dressed like the others, casually with an apron around his torso and a handkerchief tied around his forehead.

"Hey, Saddo," Mario said as he sliced carrots. "Do ya think the Syrians get along with us Italians in America?"

"Why wouldn't we? We look alike—dark skin, dark eyes."

"Your skin is almost black. I'm a devoted Italian Catholic man and you're—what?"

"I'm a Christian Greek Orthodox. I have Catholic friends back home. You think I'm black?" With each word his voice rose. "Why make a problem when there isn't one." *No one has called me black before. My temper is brewing like a thundercloud ready to burst.*

"Wait till you see a group of Italian men together. We're a tough bunch." Saddo choked back his anger. He wasn't going to risk being fired over Mario's taunts. "Let's not worry about that before it happens. Besides, haven't you heard? America is a big melting pot of different people. Now tell us something funny."

"Something funny, eh?" Mario said. "You should see my mama making her spaghetti. *That* is funny. She looks like a poma tomato wrapped up in a red apron, from her neck to the floor. Yessir. She don't wanta get dirty making her special sauce. Man, it's *deliziosa*."

They were all laughing when Juan Severino walked into the kitchen. "Glad to see you enjoying each other," he told them. "Now get on with the broth. It's almost time to serve lunch. Although, with all this rocking and rolling, I don't think many of our passengers will want to eat. Especially those poor souls in steerage."

The chef was right. Only five people occupied the dining room. But the fact that Emma appeared among them made Saddo ecstatic. As he took away her empty plate, she asked, "Saddo, may I help by asking passengers in steerage if they want hot tea?"

"How kind of you to offer. First, I need to check with Chef Juan. Wait here. I'll be right back." On the way to the kitchen, Saddo said a little prayer for the chef's approval. If Emma were to help, surely he would see even more of her.

But Juan Severino's reply was blunt. Saddo returned to Emma's side and told her quietly, "Chef Juan told me to tell you he appreciates your offer to help, but it's policy that first-class passengers not mingle with those in steerage. . . . It doesn't seem fair, does it?" He hoped that the disappointment on her face signaled, in part at least, a similar wish that they could be together.

"No, not fair at all," she said. "I'm surprised, since I don't think of myself as that different simply because I was able to travel in first class."

"In the kitchen we've talked about clashes between different cultures. Conflict seems to exist even on the passenger ships." The uncomfortable memory came back and, without thinking, Saddo started sharing it with this woman he barely knew. "One of my fellow workers, an Italian, said that my skin is almost black. This worries me. America is the land of the free. Yet I've heard of the prejudice against Negroes there. What if I'm mistaken for one?" In the distance, Juan Severino's raised voice could be heard. "I have to get back to work. Will you meet me this evening after dinner on the deck?"

"Yes, Saddo. I'll see you then. And try not to worry until you have to."

The kitchen workers spent the afternoon serving tea and broth to those who could manage to drink them. The captain and his crew, experienced with seasickness, worked to keep the ship as clean as possible. Yet it was hard, especially when the steamer plowed through heavy seas, as it did today. Saddo welcomed the break in his cabin, when he could rest before serving dinner. Lying on the narrow bed, he thought back to the day he'd left Beirut. *That first leg of the voyage was easy, with beautiful views of the calm, blue-green*

Mediterranean. The image of the sea and the coastline will forever be in my mind. What's next? . . . I wanted to punch Mario when he called me black.

As soon as his dinner shift ended, he met Emma at the steps. After she assured him that her health remained unchanged, she said, "Tell me about your journey from Beirut to Marseilles."

Saddo sighed. "I still see myself waving goodbye to my parents as the ship pulled away. It was a French steamer, designed only to make runs from Beirut to Marseilles. During the trip I helped my compatriots practice the English language. In the evenings we sang, accompanied by our ouds and darbukas. On the final evening, I thought, 'This may be the last time I'll be among so many Syrians.'"

"I think I felt the same way travelling from Dublin to Marseilles. I'll miss my parents but, unlike you, I have relatives to live with in New York City. My cousin and I are like sisters." Just then, they were interrupted by shouts from the deck. Emma and Saddo stood up and looked out the door in time to see a dozen stars plummet into the ocean.

"They always make me smile," Saddo said quietly.

"Me, too," said Emma. After a few more minutes of silence, she said, "I'm curious. How did you learn to speak English?"

"In my school, American missionaries taught it. We all learned to speak it well. Some of the men I sailed with didn't have the opportunity to learn the language. They were older than I and, like my father, spoke mostly Arabic—although my father does speak broken English and some French, since he deals with many French merchants in Aleppo."

Emma stood up. "I'm getting stiff sitting on this step. Let's walk." They continued to talk about America and their dreams for the future until dusk turned to night. The seas had calmed, and they were closer to American waters. Leaning against the rail, they said goodnight. She'd turned to leave when Saddo said, "I enjoy talking to you, Emma. I hope we can continue our friendship in America."

"I'd like that."

He stayed leaning against the rail, gazing across the dark water. *She's different from the Syrian women who have hair and eyes as dark as black onyx and skin like tawny smooth silk. Yet I feel something—but then I have feelings for Zawhea too.*

So that evening in his cramped cabin he thought of Zawhea. Saddo's sister Amina had been good friends with Zawhea since childhood. Both families belonged to the same Syrian Orthodox Church where Amina's wedding had taken place just days before Saddo left home. Zawhea and her parents of course were at the ceremony and the gathering in the church hall that followed, as were many of Saddo's and Amina's other friends. He remembered Zawhea, in a dress of midnight blue, a white sash around her waist and her long, dark hair swinging as she laughed and danced the *Al-Shamaliyya*. She attracted the attention of many young men, including Saddo. In fact, he couldn't keep his eyes off her as he joined the line of dancers. At one point, the two of them stopped dancing to eat wedding cake. They talked about his move to America, keeping the conversation lighthearted. As the celebration ended, he'd kissed both her cheeks and said he would write to her from the other side of the Atlantic.

2

Three days later Saddo woke at dawn and went to the upper deck. Yawning, rolling up shirtsleeves on his muscular arms, he looked up and admired the towering masts against the streaked sky. He smiled as he thought about his small fishing boat at home, and once more he marveled at the size of the S.S. *Neustria*. He blinked his eyes and pinched his cheek to see if this was real. Then he felt fueled with excitement. *How long have I been dreaming about this day?*

He remembered his parents' praise of their friend Anthony Abraham for going to America, and their conviction that America was a wonderful opportunity for young people. Now he, at seventeen, was about to disembark from a ship and go through Ellis Island.

He knew he had left his country weeks ago, but exactly when? From his pocket he pulled the tattered journal he'd started when the ship left Marseilles. That was twenty-two days ago. By his count, today was June 5, 1905.

As Saddo ran his hands through his curly hair, he gazed into the thickness of the clouds. Dozens of questions ran through his head like fishes swimming in a stream. *Will I be accepted? What will the people be like? Will I make friends? Calm down. This is stupid. I have positive qualities, right? I'm a Syrian Christian. I studied English at the best schools, run by local scholars with help from the American missionaries. I apprenticed with my father and have good manners and business sense. . . . But will people think I'm black because of my dark complexion?* He felt that with his enticing smile and pleasant manner he would be able to attract many friends in America, just as he did back home.

But would he? Once again, he thought about Emma—then he murmured to no one, "I have my whole future ahead of me."

By now, the sun had come up, its light turning the waves golden. At his first glimpse of the Statue of Liberty, Saddo rubbed his eyes in disbelief. She looked like a real woman waving to welcome him to the Golden Land. The rolling of the ship had stopped as the water became calm, almost as if

Libertas had said to the waves, "Here they are, about to land. Quiet down, and let them enjoy the coming."

The closer the S.S. *Neustria* came to the harbor, the more Saddo could see. He spotted Ellis Island, where he knew from Anthony Abraham's instructions that he would register for entry into his new country. Soon he realized he wasn't alone. Emma was by his side, and they were surrounded by the other passengers cheering for the new opportunities that awaited them on that American shore.

"Saddo, just look. We're here."

"Finally we made it. Let's meet after we register. Maybe by the ferry landing?"

In a short time, the ship docked. The mood on deck shifted. Some people continued to scream with joy. Others had grown quiet, possibly from feelings of fear, uncertainty, or both.

Saddo was surprised at how orderly the passengers, despite their emotions, disembarked onto waiting barges. He was certain that every man, woman, and child shared his desire to be on firm ground again.

The barges transported them across the Hudson River to Ellis Island. At close range, the building looked like a castle. At the entrance the American flag flew high above the ground. Saddo walked off with the others toward the Great Hall.

Once inside, Saddo gasped at the number of people trying to enter this country. *Will there be room enough for us all?* The odors coming from thousands of insufficiently washed bodies, including his own, made him feel light-headed for a few seconds.

Officials pinned an identification tag on him, as they did on all the other new arrivals. It showed the number given to him when he boarded the S.S. *Neustria*. Then the clerks, trained to manage the crowds, directed everyone to the second floor. There, Saddo knew, the registration would begin with a medical check, because understandably the Americans didn't want pests or diseases brought into the country. Saddo was nervous, but at least he understood the process, and for this he silently thanked Anthony Abraham.

He immediately noticed the sign "To Registry Room" and began the climb up two flights of stairs. Stopping at the top, he turned to the woman behind him. She held a baby wrapped in a heavy blanket. "Can you believe we're here?" Saddo told her. "I've never seen a room this large. And look at the American flags at each end."

"Yes, it's our new country," she said. "Well, almost." Saddo couldn't tell from the woman's dress or accent where she was from. But at this point, it didn't matter.

The baby started to fuss. "Would you like help with your little one?" Saddo asked. "I have time."

The young woman looked relieved as she carefully gave the baby to Saddo.

He held the child while she dug in her coat pockets.

They continued to wait. Finally, it was their turn. Since men went into one room for the physical exam, and women and their children went into another, Saddo handed the baby back to its mother and wished her well. She nodded again.

The first room he entered was to check for lice. He bent over as the doctor combed through his hair. Only then did he realize how long it had grown during the voyage.

"Sir, you have no lice," an official told him. "Go forward for your eye exam."

Scratching his head not for lice, but in wonder at how he'd avoided being infested with them on the ship, Saddo headed to the next room. There, a doctor used an instrument resembling a buttonhole hook to check under his eyelids. Saddo grimaced for a second then looked up, down, and around. It was over quickly and with little pain.

"Sir, your eyes are good," the doctor announced.

With this news, Saddo wanted to run down the stairs. But he contained himself, walking to the first floor and entering the Great Hall again, this time for final questioning. Now he had a chance to really look around, and what he saw amazed him. If he'd needed to, he could have bought a train ticket, exchanged money, sent a telegraph, and been seated for a meal along with three thousand others in the dining room—all in the same enormous space. Saddo's amazement at the scale of Americans' endeavors was increasing by the minute.

He was in line for the questions—questions that determined immigrants' legitimacy and also served to weed out troublemakers—when he felt a tap on his back. He turned to the elderly man behind him and said, "Can I help you?

The man was trembling. "What will they ask me and what do I say?"

"Remember what they told us on the ship. Show them your money, tell

18

them where you're going and that you have a job waiting or a family to care for you. They might ask if you're an anarchist. Or a criminal. Say no." Saddo's heart went out to the man, now shaking harder than before. "I'll stay with you to help—in case you don't understand the questions."

"Thank you, sir. After a long journey, I forget. My daughter will meet me where I get my trunk back. She lives in Manhattan."

"Please, move in front of me."

With a level of patience that impressed Saddo, the clerk recorded the old man's name, the date of his arrival and on which ship, his place of origin, his language, his age, and the family members already in America. A short time later, though, the clerk's patience stalled a bit when it came time to record his own name: "Saddo Ibn Hanna." Saddo offered his father's middle name, Samuel, as a replacement for the first name he'd been baptized with. Then he slowly spelled his last name for the clerk. So, in a matter of seconds, Saddo Ibn Hanna officially became Samuel Hanna. Little did he, and all the others arriving, realize that many years later, their children, and their children's children, would visit Ellis Island Museum to look up their names.

After Saddo, now Samuel, had helped the gentleman through the ordeal, he walked him to the baggage room and made sure he located his trunk. The elderly man shook Samuel's hand, saying, "I now wait for my daughter."

Samuel picked up his own bag and walked out of the building. He took one last glance at its magnificence then headed toward the ferry, hoping to find Emma. The guards had assembled three lines, formed in the order in which people came out of the building, and each line inched forward to board the ferry. He frantically scanned the crowd for Emma, but with no luck. Then, only a few yards from the boarding point, he heard her voice. "Saddo, please wait."

He quickly moved back to join her. He could tell from Emma's relaxed face that she'd sailed smoothly through all the questioning. "There you are. You must call me 'Samuel' now."

"Why 'Samuel'?"

"The clerk had too much trouble with 'Saddo.' So I took my father's middle name as my first name."

They boarded the same ferry and headed across the water to the big city, once again passing the Statue of Liberty. Outwardly, Samuel smiled and made small talk with Emma. Inwardly he was trembling, and he couldn't help but think of the elderly gentleman anticipating the clerk's questions. *I*

*have no idea what to do next, except to look for Mr. Abraham's sign of greeting. And to
pray that no one calls me black.*

Once they'd arrived in Manhattan, Samuel knew he had to open his heart
to Emma. He pulled her aside on the dusty American street, crowded with
carriages, trolley cars, and an inconceivable number of people. Samuel
whispered, "I'll find a way to see you again." Her response, a coy smile and
flushed cheeks, confused him. But this wasn't the time or place to ask
anything of her.

Besides, he knew he had to stick with his plan to begin his merchant
apprenticeship. He owed that much to his parents, since they had arranged
for Anthony Abraham to provide him guidance in America. In the end,
Emma and Samuel agreed that he would try to return to New York City in a
few months for a visit and, in the meantime, they'd write to each other and
continue to sort out their feelings.

As they walked together, Samuel heard a man mutter, disgust in his voice,
"Look at that Negro with the white woman." Samuel approached the man
with a raised fist.

Emma held him back. "Saddo . . . Samuel, we talked about this. Be calm
if you can and pay no attention."

"You may think that's easy. Your skin is white."

At that moment, they heard the ecstatic shriek of a woman close by. She
held a sign on which "Emma Monahan" was written in a fancy script. Emma
and the woman fell into each other's arms. Samuel remained where he was,
observing, astounded by the resemblance between Emma and her cousin
Bernadette. They had the same fair skin, the same blue eyes, the same
auburn hair. The cousin led Emma toward an older man, who welcomed her
with a more modest hug.

Emma began talking so fast that her cousin said, "Slow down, my dear. I
can barely understand you." Her voice had an unusual booming quality
which surprised Samuel since Emma's voice was so soft and pleasant.

Emma picked up where she'd left off, then seconds later she stopped.
"What's your address?" As her cousin started to answer, Emma interrupted
her. "Write it down, please."

Her cousin, clearly puzzled, took paper and pencil from her reticule.
Samuel's observation of Emma ended when he heard someone call out
"Saddo Hanna?" Not far from Emma and her relatives stood Anthony

20

Abraham, holding a sign with Samuel's former name on it. Samuel walked over to the man with his hand outstretched.

Anthony Abraham hugged him instead and said, "Welcome to America." Then he stepped back and looked at Samuel from head to toe. "You're a man now. No wonder I was a bit uncertain. . . . And your family?"

"All healthy when I left them, sir. They send their regards."

"Well, Saddo, at this point you'd probably rather stay put for a while. But of course I have to get you to your final destination. We'll take the trolley to catch the train from Penn Station to Union Station in Pittsburgh. Then we'll spend the night with my brother Saehan and continue on to New Salem in the morning. My buggy and horses are in his care."

"I remember Saehan from his last visit to Damascus. . . . By the way, I'm now Samuel Hanna. 'Saddo' seemed to be a problem for the officials." He pointed vaguely in the direction of Ellis Island. "Fortunately, my father's middle name sounds more American. Agreed?" "Yes. But I may slip occasionally. Please remind me, Samuel."

Samuel looked toward Emma. "Do I have time to say goodbye to someone?"

"Of course," Anthony said. But he raised his eyebrows when he saw who the "someone" was. He followed Samuel.

"Emma, this is my dear family friend, Mr. Abraham," Samuel began the introductions. "We're about ready to begin our journey."

"I'm pleased to meet you, sir," she replied, lowering her eyes. "This is my cousin Bernadette and our uncle, John Gutwald." She slipped Samuel a piece of paper.

His eyes lit up as he read the address. Close to her ear, he said, "As soon as I'm settled, I'll write to you. Look for a letter. We'll meet again." Feeling uncharacteristically heedless, he touched Emma's arm, though slightly, and then they parted ways.

3

Peering through the grimy window, Samuel found it hard to sit still, despite his exhaustion. "Mr. Abraham, someday I'll return your kindness."

"*Mr. Abraham?* Please, call me Anthony. Remember, I'm only ten years older than you. And I think of you as a brother." He patted Samuel on the back. "I remember the days you helped your father and me. You'll do well. As for repaying me, let's talk about that later."

Samuel touched his bag stored under the seat, glad once again that he had traveled so leanly. He thought back to the chaotic scene when they'd boarded the train, and to the impatience he'd felt at the many passengers with piled-up valises and trunks. It seemed to take forever to get all the baggage loaded.

Somewhere between New York City and Pittsburgh, there was a notable change in the sky. Samuel lowered the window a bit and took a deep breath. The air was much fresher. The countryside was in full bloom. He gazed at the green hills and, against his will, a comparison came to mind: What he was passing through looked lush, but it wasn't as beautiful as the land along the Mediterranean coastline. There, olive, fig, and orange trees dotted the fields and villages.

When Anthony awoke from a short nap, he told Samuel more about New Salem. "The town sits on a small hill close to Uniontown. The coal mining communities of Footedale, Buffington, Ronco, Fairbank, and Republic surround us. I peddle my goods to them, as well as to farm families in the vicinity." He stretched out his legs. "Then there are the patch towns. Settlements that the mining companies built to give the miners a place to call home. In every patch town, you'll find a school, churches, and a few businesses, including the company store. Mind you, though, the air in those areas is thick with haze from the coal."

"Tell me about the miners."

"The miners? Although I don't envy their lot in life, I do respect them. They're very industrious and work hard to provide for their families. I really don't know how they manage the work. It's tough on the body and soul. But I gather that, among most of them, their faith is strong. Clearly, these men realize the dangers of going into the mines."

"Wait a minute. There are company stores in the patch towns? So how do you compete with them?"

"Well, the goods I have to offer aren't usually found in those stores. Also, most women find it difficult to leave the house during the day. They're busy tending to their family's needs. So they like having me come to them. . . . You'll enjoy meeting the women and the families."

Samuel grew pensive. "Do you think the people in these towns are generally happy?" He was thinking of the jovial nature of most of his friends and relatives at home.

"A good question. I would say yes, the majority are relatively happy. The coal company does look out for the people in its town. And it provides land for their churches."

Samuel tried to imagine the towns—the women, the families, the miners in heavy work boots and trousers coated with soot trudging home after work. *Sturdy clothing is needed for such work. Soon I'll be selling such clothes and more. . . .* He soon fell asleep and dreamed about his future.

Samuel woke as the train jerked to a stop at Union Station in Pittsburgh. Anthony's brother Saehan was waiting for them. Anyone seeing the three men standing on the station platform would have thought all of them were brothers, not just two. They had the same dark olive skin, curly black hair, and deep brown eyes, and all three wore similar loose-fitting pants, suspenders, and brown shirts.

Over the shrill whistles of trains and the hubbub of the crowd around them, Anthony introduced Samuel. "Saehan, do you remember meeting Samuel? Except that you knew him as Saddo then."

"Yes, of course," Saehan replied. "I last saw you at your home in Damascus. When was it, eh? Five years ago? Well, we've been awaiting your arrival. You must be weary after such a long journey."

"Yes, sir. It was very long. But I had no problems along the way, and for that I'm thankful. Many of the passengers became ill and weak."

"Good to hear you weren't downed with illness," said Saehan. "You must be a robust young man."

Saehan led his brother and Samuel outside the station, where his buggy was parked. "Hop in," he told Samuel. "My home isn't far from here. Soon you'll have food and rest. Tomorrow, before you leave for New Salem, I'll show you the wholesale district. That's where I work as a jobber."

"A jobber?" asked Samuel.

"Manufacturers sell direct to me, and I sell the goods to peddlers and storeowners. You could say I'm the middleman between the wholesalers and retail."

The next morning, after eating hot Syrian bread with za'atar prepared by Saehan's wife, the three men went to Fifth Avenue Uptown—the wholesale district. Samuel absorbed every detail of the unfamiliar surroundings, and he closely watched in fascination as Anthony made the deals, purchasing workpants, shirts, boots, jackets, undergarments, fabric, needles, threads, and housedresses.

Their next stop was a Syrian market on Fifth Avenue to buy spices. Breathing in the smell of fresh cinnamon, Samuel picked up a few cinnamon sticks and sighed, thinking of home. He listened to Anthony explain that he sold the spices to the grocer in New Salem, after setting some aside for his own family and friends. Samuel was in awe. *So this is the way they conduct deals for the business. I hope someday I can make the trips to Pittsburgh myself.*

After lunch, Anthony and Samuel said their goodbyes to Saehan and his wife. Anthony had Samuel admire his horses before climbing onto the two-seated buggy, which had a back seat for transporting goods. As they pulled away, Anthony said, "It's tough to make the trip to New Salem in one day. We travel the National Pike, which has some asphalt but is mostly dirt road.

Many areas are rough, and this makes it difficult for the horses to travel too long. So I stop at Sophia's boarding house in Connellsville. Sophia cooks just like our mothers and is ever so kind."

Anthony drove for several hours. By the time Samuel took a turn, rain was coming down heavily. "The horses aren't bothered by the weather," he said, "but I'm happy to have a roof over my head." Arab, the prancing dark brown horse, appeared to be in charge. Coalie, the stocky black horse snorted as he tried to keep up.

As they approached the boarding house, Samuel brought Coalie and Arab to a halt. He hitched up the horses then followed Anthony to get them water and food.

While Anthony pumped water, a short, plump woman came out onto the porch. "Anthony, so good to see you," she called.

When they'd joined her, Anthony made the introductions. Samuel took off his hat and bowed slightly. "*Shukran* for having me," he told the woman.

"Welcome to America, Samuel," Sophia said. "Come in and make yourselves comfortable. We'll soon sit down for dinner."

Anthony took a deep breath, savoring the smells drifting in from the kitchen. "You must be cooking *kibbeh*."

The aroma of onions, cinnamon, mint, and pine nuts brought tears to Samuel's eyes. *It smells like my umm's kitchen.* He watched as Anthony pulled a small box from his pack and hand it to Sophia.

"My spices, you dear man. Thank you for your trouble."

"You know it's no trouble," Anthony replied. "I enjoy bringing you this small gift. Your boarding house is pleasant and gives me the time to rest."

"Dinner will be ready soon. You can relax in the parlor—oh, and you're my only guests this evening."

After dinner, Samuel and Anthony went straight to bed, although Samuel would have liked to hear more of Sophia's stories. He tossed and turned in the unfamiliar surroundings, and he woke up out of an unsettling dream right when the sun began to rise.

After a hearty breakfast, Sophia sent them on their way with two fresh loaves of Syrian bread, still warm. As soon as they were on the road, they looked at each other then tore into the bread, savoring the taste as each bite melted in their mouth.

While they continued toward western Pennsylvania, Samuel told Anthony about his dream. "I was on a crowded city street lined with speakeasies and hotels. All of a sudden, I found myself surrounded by a daunting group of Italian men. They called me blackie . . . and nigger. Everywhere I turned, there was another one. I was screaming at them in Arabic, throwing punches at the closer ones. I found myself running through the crowd looking for a safe place. Then everything shifted, and I was in my home in Damascus. But instead of getting to spend time there, I woke up, confused and worried about where I was. I told myself it was only a dream."

Anthony said, "Right. It was only a dream. Yet, sadly, what you experienced in it does happen. This is why you'll see that in the big cities we settle in communities of our own. Now, in New Salem there's a mix of culture, but we're very accepting of each other—although at times the Polish and Italians working in the mines will go at each other."

The forest Samuel was passing through fell away, replaced by the scene in the ship's kitchen. "I worked with two Italian men on the ship," he said. "One of them, Mario, taunted me about the color of my skin. Then, in Manhattan, while I was waiting to meet you a man called me black. I was ready to explode." "Samuel, listen to the advice of someone who's been in America for a while. You don't want to explode—or even come close to exploding—if you can help it. This is true no matter what your business is. But it's especially true if you're in the peddling business. The good news is that I haven't experienced anything bad in New Salem in all these years. . . . Samuel, have you heard me?"

He slowly nodded.

"Good," said Anthony. "Now let's talk of happier things. Sadie and Tony are anxious to see you and to have you with us. My son is five years old now. I can hardly believe it. Every day he's been asking, 'When is Saddo coming?' You remember meeting Sadie at your home, before we married. A year after I arrived here, Sadie and her mother came to America. At first they stayed in Pittsburgh with Sadie's brother. Then, once I could arrange to bring Sadie to New Salem, we married." His broad smile told Samuel that the man was still very much in love with his wife. "Our home is small, but you'll have your own bedroom. For months now, Sadie has been fussing over your coming. And of course she's hungry for news from home."

They'd just left Uniontown, and on a narrow, bumpy, winding dirt road they headed up the hill toward New Salem. With a deep sigh, Samuel let the dream go completely. He replaced it with the thought of Emma picking up the bottom of her skirt as she stepped up into her uncle's buggy, just before they went to the dock to pick up her two trunks. *How can women have so many clothes? Her father owns the Cruises Royal Hotel, her mother designs lace, and her uncle manages the Hotel Wolcott. Maybe that explains the clothes.*

They arrived in New Salem just as it turned dark. The sky revealed a slice of moon and lightly dancing stars. Samuel welcomed the cooler air, since the day had been warm and sticky. They drove down Center Street to the opposite edge of town. On the corner was a white clapboard house, and on the steps leading up to its front porch sat Sadie and Tony. Samuel quickly saw that Anthony had been right about his family's anticipation. Little Tony had a big grin on his face, and Sadie, after rubbing her hands on her apron, gave him a hug and exclaimed, "I'm happy you're finally here! How is your wonderful family?"

"They're healthy and send their love," Samuel replied. "My sister Amina married Zacharias Rahal a few days before I left. They live in Aleppo, where he works in silk exports, helping my father with the business."

"All good news," said Sadie. "You're fortunate that your father is a successful businessman. You learned from the best."

Later, as they sat around the table after dinner, Tony listened intently while Samuel talked about his journey. "My family and friends were sad to see me leave. I'll miss them." His face brightened. "There were people from many countries on the ship. I met one girl, Emma, who was traveling from Ireland to live with family in New York City." He remembered the address on the piece of paper still in a pocket. "Actually, in Brooklyn. Many evenings after I finished my work in the kitchen, we would meet on the deck and talk about our countries. She's very different from my friends at home—from her hair to the clothes she wears and the food she likes."

Anthony said gently, sounding exactly like an older brother, "Samuel, it's good you begin to think about other cultures, since America truly is the melting pot people call it. We do have customs from our dear Syria that differ from those of other countries—you already know that from the many merchants that came to Aleppo. We have a close Syrian community here in New Salem, and you'll find it easy to make new friends through our work—and through the church as well."

"What's the name of the church here?" asked Samuel.

"St. George Syrian Orthodox. We built it with funds from the Pittsburgh Diocese and community members. For now we have a visiting priest."

Sadie apparently was still thinking about the crossing. "You're so handsome and smart. I'm not surprised you met a young woman on the ship."

Samuel blushed in response.

Tony yawned, and Sadie picked him up. "Come now. Time for bed. Why don't you show Samuel his room?"

Tony bounced down from his mother's arms and scampered up the steps. Samuel followed. On the way up, Tony said, "*Umm* told me your name is Saddo."

"Now I have two names. One for Syria and one for America. Samuel is my American name."

27

"I like your American name better."

Tony went inside the room to the left of the stair landing. It was furnished with a single bed, chest of drawers, and side chair. The warm evening air coming in through the window gently blew the bright blue curtains. The window faced the back of the house and overlooked the barn where Anthony kept his goods.

Samuel sat down on the bed. Tony jumped up beside him and said, "Can I sleep with you tonight?"

Samuel shook his head. "How about on a night when I don't have to wake up early for work?"

"Maybe Saturday." Tony grinned. "You can be my big brother. Okay?" "I can be," Samuel said. He already felt himself settling into his new life, feeling at peace.

4

Samuel's first week in New Salem sped by in whirlwind fashion. He reviewed Anthony's business plan. He learned about the customers, their languages and home countries, and any other details about them that Anthony felt important.

On Saturday afternoon they went into town. It was an easy walk to the markets. Samuel wanted to get to know the people who worked and lived in New Salem. There was the grocer's market that sold food, sundries, books, toys, and the daily Uniontown newspapers, the *Morning Herald* and the *Evening Standard*. A tin shop and carpenter shop stood side by side. Across the street were the barbershop and the inn with a tavern. Beside the inn was a tiny building that housed the post office and the local constable.

It being a Saturday, many people wandered about shopping. By the end of the afternoon, Samuel felt as if he'd met them all. Anthony also took him to every shop to meet the owners. With one of them, John Nazzif, who had the carpenter shop, Samuel felt an instant connection—though if anyone had asked him why, he couldn't have explained it.

"Welcome. Anthony told me you'd be arriving," John greeted him. "I came just a couple of years ago from Aleppo. If you're still nearby when I close the shop, we can meet at the tavern and have a drink."

"I'd like that. See you there," he replied.

Anthony and Samuel continued to visit the other merchants until it was time for the shops to close. Then Samuel told Anthony, "This has been a good day for me. I've been here a short time, and yet I already feel like part of the community. Shall we meet John at the tavern?"

"Sadie is expecting me. You young men enjoy yourselves."

At the tavern, it didn't take long for Samuel to realize why he'd felt the connection with John. The carpenter described his voyage from Aleppo, and his life and work in Syria and New Salem. Their experiences, their religion and culture, their business ideas all had a great deal in common. John even played the darbuka.

29

THE SYRIAN PEDDLER

The first month went by quickly, just as the first week had, with Samuel peddling merchandise to the customers in New Salem, the neighboring villages, and the surrounding countryside. He enjoyed meeting the people, and he began to teach himself their languages—Slovak, Polish, and Hungarian—since many of them hadn't learned English. He was always happy to speak Arabic with his Syrian customers. As the days passed, Anthony, seeing what a fast learner Samuel was, gave him more and more responsibility.

One evening, while thinking about his new country and his new work, Samuel realized he hadn't written to Zawhea. He immediately looked for a pen and paper.

July 15, 1905
Dear Zawhea,
What a voyage I had! I cannot begin to relate the entire story in writing. Yet I will give you some details so you might have an idea of what I experienced. My cabin was clean, small with a porthole, and I was able to sleep comfortably. A few days after we left Marseilles, I heard that the head chef needed extra help. So I asked about it and he hired me. The job kept me busy and gave me extra liras, or, as they say here, dollars. I worked side by side with several men from other countries and mainly served dinner in the first-class dining room. One day, though, I helped serve tea to the ill passengers in steerage, so I was able to see their living arrangements. They slept in large rooms on cots, in very dark and dingy quarters where the air was still and stuffy. Families from the same country stayed together. If you make the voyage—which I pray you do—please purchase a first-class ticket. Very few of us traveling in first class became sick.
We had such a celebration here on July 4, the American Independence Day. There was a picnic and a parade with a band. The day ended with all the townspeople singing "My Country 'Tis of Thee," with cannon shots in the background. That day I understood the joy people have about their freedom and the democracy of this

country. It was then that I began planning to become a naturalized citizen.

Anthony and Sadie are very kind to me, and their son Tony is like a little brother. I am happy here with my work, and I enjoy the community of New Salem. Each morning I awake looking forward to new opportunities.

I often think about Amina's wedding and the dancing. It is a wonderful memory of our last time together.
Salaam,
Saddo

5

One day in early August, Samuel and Anthony were doing inventory and making a list of what to purchase on the next buying trip. Halfway through the task, Anthony asked Samuel, "Will you go to Pittsburgh for me?

I want to be home when Tony starts school."

Samuel, surprised by the question and by the trust Anthony had come to have in him in such a short time, replied, "Of course" and smiled.

"I knew you would," said Anthony. "I can see you're a quick learner. In fact, I'd like you to keep track of our inventory in the future."

Another surprise followed. Anthony suggested that Samuel go to Brooklyn to see Emma on the same trip. He could stay with Anthony's friends, the Nadars. Right away, Samuel wrote to Emma asking if he could visit her in September. If she agreed, his plan would be to spend time with her before he purchased the goods.

One Saturday morning, not long after he'd posted the letter, Samuel stood before the living room window, looking out at the people passing by. He heard Tony sneak up behind him, then felt the boy's little arms around his legs. Samuel reacted as he always did in this game of theirs. He turned around with a jump and lifted Tony as high as he could. And, as always, the game ended with laughter bubbling out of both of them. *Life is good, here in the house of this warm and kind family. I do miss my own family, but my father was right about America. It's great to be here. . . . If only the letters wouldn't take so long to arrive.*

September came quickly. The days grew cooler, and the leaves were beginning to lose their gleaming green luster, to be replaced with blotches of yellow and brown. Anthony and Samuel were traveling in the buggy from New Salem to the newly opened train station in Uniontown.

"This is wonderful, isn't it?" said Anthony. "No longer having to take Arab and Coalie the hundred miles to Pittsburgh. Better for them and better for us."

"Wait until we have our automobiles," Samuel said. "I dream of owning one soon. Father has one, and we used to work together on it. I thought about becoming a mechanic. But I believe business is the better of the two careers."

"You learned from the best—your father. Purchasing an automobile is a dream for most of us. As for me, first I'll open my own store."

On a warm evening, Samuel arrived in Brooklyn and followed Anthony's directions to George Nadar's home. Walking along Atlantic Avenue, he saw many people who looked much like him and his friends back home. There were no single homes on the avenue—only rows of plain grey or brown apartment buildings. Grass was scarce. Children played tag in the middle of the street.

He walked up the front steps and rang the bell at number 1942. An older man answered the door and welcomed him with a hug. "You must be Samuel," he said. "Come in. I'm George Nadar." With a hand on Samuel's shoulder, he guided him into the front room, where children were on the floor playing marbles.

After Samuel had met the family, he joined the men. Pausing to look around, he had the sudden sensation of being wrapped in a warm, cozy blanket. That was the effect of the comfortable padded chairs, the sofa with pillows of colors seen on stained-glass windows in their churches. He took in the familiar aromas of his favorite foods. *This is just like Sundays at my home I understand why they call this Little Syria.*

When dinner was ready, everyone sat down in the dozen high back chairs around the large, rectangular oak table in the middle of the kitchen.

George Nadar spoke softly, giving thanks for their many blessings. Then the conversation began, a mixture of Arabic and English, as the food was passed around. At the same time, everyone tore pieces of bread from the round loaves and dipped them in oil and za'atar.

George asked Samuel to describe his work in New Salem.

"Well, Anthony and I travel the patch towns near the coal mines selling our merchandise. The business is good, but so very different from working in the city." Samuel paused. "My dream is to open my own dry goods store in a small town where families can come to me to shop."

"My boy, you have an ambitious dream," George said. "Don't give it up. I never gave up my dream when I arrived in Brooklyn. And now look at me."

George's wife, Rose, glanced at her husband. Then she turned to Samuel and said quietly, "So you're here to call on a young lady?"

"Yes. I met Emma on the ship coming over," replied Samuel. "She's living with her uncle and aunt in Brooklyn. An Irish settlement, as I'm sure you know."

He saw George nod to his wife. Then she said, "When you call on her tomorrow, you can invite her to join us for dinner."

Samuel tried to hide his surprise. "How kind of you."

Samuel practically hopped down George's steps, shining in the mid-morning sunlight, and quickly bought flowers at the corner shop. Then at a fast clip he headed for the trolley stop.

From his seat in the back of the trolley, he looked at the other passengers. Some were dark-skinned, others light-skinned, still others had shades of skin between dark and light. Green eyes, grey eyes, blue eyes, and eyes so dark they appeared black. Curly, wavy, and straight hair of half a dozen colors. Clothing that hinted at a dozen different countries. *America truly is a melting pot.* Yet, although Samuel was now a part of this melting pot, as the trolley approached his stop, he started to get the jitters. *I don't want to be insulted ever again for the color of my skin.*

A few blocks from the trolley stop, he found 2014 Gaelic Street, the home of John and Agnes Gutwald. He knocked and waited, shifting from one foot to the other, checking to see if his tie was straight.

The woman who opened the door had to be Emma's aunt. "Welcome, Samuel. I'm Mrs. Gutwald. How nice to meet you. Come in."

"Pleased to meet you, Mrs. Gutwald." Samuel handed her the bouquet of pink and white carnations from behind his back and bowed at the waist.

"You do know how to make an impression, young man. Obviously, your mother raised you to be a gentleman. Please go sit in the drawing room. I'll let Emma know you're here."

Samuel sat down on a high back cane chair and looked around. The uncomfortable chair fit in with the room's sparse décor, a dark brown sofa and one other cane chair. The only object of adornment was a painting of the Blessed Virgin Mary above the fireplace. The drawing room was dreary compared to the brightness of the cloudless, blue September sky outside the window—and also dreary compared to the soft-cushion chairs, the gold pillows, and colorful paintings in his family's home in Damascus.

It wasn't long before Emma walked in. "Samuel, you really are here. I'm sorry I kept you waiting."

He stood up and gave her a nervous hug. "Emma, you look as lovely as I remember."

They both started to talk at the same time. Laughing, he said, "Tell me what you've been doing since we last were together."

That was all Emma needed to hear. She launched into a long speech about the lacemaking and her dream to open a lace shop in the city. "The shop's name will be Limerick Irish Lace Designs by BernEm, owned by Bernadette Kimlin and Emma Monahan. Can't you picture the sign hanging over the entrance? For now, we're able to sell our designs to tailors Uncle John knows. We're even beginning to make lace pendants."

Samuel tried to concentrate on Emma's words. But eventually his mind wandered. *She's very driven to have her own business. Most of the women I know love working in their homes. And they meet in each other's homes to bake bread while they share stories about raising their children. About helping their husbands in the family business. They sometimes even keep the books. Samuel's thoughts hit a wall. But these are the Syrian women of my mother's generation. The younger women, much more progressive, are planning to attend university.*

A servant announcing lunch interrupted Emma. She led Samuel to the dining room. Bernadette and Emma's uncle had taken time away from their work at the hotel to join them. The conversation centered on their business and on the Irish community. As Samuel listened, he made an effort to eat the food in front of him. The main dish, called an Irish stew, consisted of a broth with beef, potatoes, carrots, and onions. But he couldn't taste any spices, except maybe a little garlic. And the soda bread was dry. *The food is bland—not much taste or seasoning to it.*

After lunch, Emma and Samuel took the trolley to visit the Hotel Wolcott. Walking along West Thirty-First Street, they talked about their voyage. Samuel started to feel the old comfort he'd had with Emma on the ship. The two of them were lost in the crowd of shoppers and other people pursuing their daily routine in the city. Samuel described his life in New Salem.

"You're happy," Emma remarked.

35

"I am. I love the work and the community. At times I miss my family and home. But the opportunities here are abundant."

They stopped in front of the hotel. Emma pointed to a building across the street. "See that? It's the Martha Washington Apartments for Professional Women. Newly opened. Bernadette and I hope to save money to move there."

"Emma, that seems unusual—young women living alone in New York City."

"It is. This is the first apartment for women in the city. But at least there's a housemother."

"A new American way," he replied.

When they entered the hotel, Samuel marveled at the modern French architecture and the sculptured decorations. He looked up at the multicolored stained-glass window over the first landing of the staircase. It reminded him of the church window in Damascus he knew so well. Emma started the tour beginning in the lobby, going to the café, the dining room, the smoking room, and ending in the large main drawing room called the Palm Room. High French mirrors, stained glass, ornamental iron, mosaic floors, mahogany chairs with velvet upholstery . . . the effect was stunning.

Samuel remembered the piano he'd seen during the tour. "Does someone play music to entertain guests in the café?" he asked.

"I do," Emma replied. "Three times a week during the noon lunch hours and before dinner. I love that I can keep playing here in America."

"Yes. I remember you mentioning your piano lessons in Limerick. Please play for me before we leave."

"Let's stop by Uncle John's office. We'll say hello and see if it would be okay."

Her uncle quickly gave his approval, and a few minutes later Emma was playing "My Wild Irish Rose." Many of the guests stopped their conversation to listen. Samuel leaned forward in awe to hear each note as Emma's fingers moved delicately across the keys. He was touched by the melody, picturing her as the loveliest rose in a garden. When she completed the piece, he clapped the loudest.

After saying goodbye to Emma's uncle, they continued on to George Nadar's shop. Their plan was to take the trolley with him to have dinner at the Nadars.

An hour later, Samuel again found himself in the kitchen with George's family—this time sitting beside Emma.

When the bread was passed, Emma said, "Samuel, would you like me to slice a piece for you?"

He smiled. "When you eat Syrian bread, you don't slice it. You just tear a piece off the round loaf, then dip it in olive oil and in this savory Syrian spice called za'atar." She looked down at her plate, blushing. Hoping to put her at ease, he dipped a piece of the bread in the oil and za'atar and offered it. "Try this," he said as gently as he could.

"Delicious," Emma said with her mouth half full. "The bread and the flavors of the oil and spice together are simply delicious." With that comment, everyone went back to eating and talking.

Later, Rose's younger daughter brought dates to the table. Her older daughter brought a plate of *baklava*. Even from where he sat, Samuel detected the scent of the orange-blossom syrup used to make the traditional pastry. Rose served *ahweh*—the strong, sweet, cardamom-flavored coffee that put to shame most of the "American" coffee he had tasted. Then she asked Emma about her life in Ireland. The daughters' wide-eyed looks suggested they shared their mother's curiosity. Emma began to describe her home and family hotel in Limerick.

Samuel found himself paying less attention to Emma and more to George, as he talked about his business and what it was like being Syrian in the city. "My life is centered on my shop, my family, and my Syrian friends in the community. Not so different, really, from the time before I came to America." Samuel looked intently at George. *This is what I want for myself as my business grows in New Salem.*

It was getting on toward nine o'clock. Emma offered to help with the dishes, but Rose thought she and Samuel should start back before it was too late.

When they got off the trolley, Samuel saw Emma's home from the stop. He hugged her. "It's been wonderful spending time with you again. And getting to hear you play. Someday we might be playing the darbuka and piano together."

He could feel her heart beating against his chest, and he bent over to give her a gentle kiss on the cheek.

Emma backed away. Still, she said, "That was sweet." He walked her to the door. "I'll write you."

"It *was* nice to see you. And, yes, please write soon."

Samuel was halfway to the street when he heard Bernadette's voice come from behind the opened door. "I want to hear all about it," she told Emma, "and don't tell Aunt Agnes I said this, but she remarked that Samuel looks black." He grimaced and hurried to the street. He wondered what Emma's reaction had been to a remark so hurtful to him.

6

The next day Samuel was in Pittsburgh, meeting with Saehan and surveying his goods. He ordered the usual work boots, rugged shirts and pants. Then his eyes were attracted to the bright colors of some suspenders off to the left.

"We'll order the same number of brown suspenders as we always do," he told Saehan. "But let's add something different this time. I'm thinking about the dreary nature of coal mining. The men and their families need more brightness in their lives. So give me the same number of those blue suspenders."

"That's something Anthony has never done," said Saehan.

"Also, add three bolts each of the floral cotton fabric and the light blue linen. And two of the ecru organza and white silk with matching spools of thread . . . say, three dozen of each. Now, could I see the dress patterns? Our women make clothes not only for the family but also for themselves. So of course they're interested in the latest fashions."

With the orders packed up, Samuel headed to the train station, his thoughts whirling. *What have I done buying extra goods? What will Anthony think? I know we'll sell them and our customers will like the choices. But, if they don't? . . . My mind has been focused on business most of this trip, and here I've just seen Emma. She's a sweet woman, but so driven to be a success. So very different from Zawhea.*

When Samuel got off the train in Uniontown, the orange and yellow leaves were swirling about. The wind also blew Samuel's curly, longer-than-usual hair. Anthony was waiting for him at the station. Samuel threw his bag in the back of the buggy, patted Coalie and Arab, and hopped up onto the seat.

Soon after they started toward New Salem, Samuel said, "I can't thank you enough for sending me on this buying trip. I learned so much from talking to George. I can hardly wait to open my own place. It'll be called Hanna's Department Store."

"Let's hope that before you open yours, I open mine. Otherwise, Sadie will be very upset with me." They both laughed.

"While I was putting together our order, I had a thought: How about new suspenders in different colors—and more fabric for the women to add to their sewing selections?" He paused. "I shouldn't say 'how about.' Actually, I bought these things. The suspenders and the thread for the fabric are in my bag. So are the new Butterick patterns. The rest of the order will arrive by freight. I hope you're not upset. In fact, I hope you're pleased with what I did."

Anthony scratched his head. "You may have made a good business decision. No, I'm definitely not upset about it. Let's see how the items sell." Anthony looked thoughtful. "I have to admit. You're a delight to work with. And I admire your ambition. Welcome home."

An hour later they reached the Abraham home. While they were hitching up the horses, Tony ran out the front door. Samuel picked him up and swung him in a circle, saying, "Hello. How's my little friend?"

Tony giggled. "I missed you."

Sadie had followed her son outside. "How was your visit with Emma?" Samuel didn't skip a beat. "We had a good time together. I'll tell you about it later. For now, I'll show you the new purchases. Close your eyes." He opened his bag. "Ready."

"Oh, Samuel!" Sadie exclaimed. "I love the bright colors. The other women will too. And these suspenders! The men will look so handsome on holidays and Sundays in these bright blue ones. I hope you bought some blue shirts."

"Yes. And bolts of fabric that match the thread are on the way." He turned to Tony. "Come see what I have for you." He reached into his bag as Tony peeked over his shoulder. "Ah, here it is. A shiny red top." Tony's eyes sparkled as he took the toy to go play on the porch.

Samuel tried to nap on the couch. But he was restless, unable to stop thinking about Emma. He went into the kitchen to find Sadie. They often talked while he helped her prepare dinner. Pulling up a chair, he said, "Anthony was kind to suggest that I visit Emma on my trip. It was good to see her again. Her aunt prepared lunch for us. But, to tell the truth, I didn't enjoy eating Irish food."

Sadie stopped chopping onions. "Is food the most important part of your friendship with Emma?"

"No, of course not. But you know that food—and music, I suppose—are at the center of any Syrian's life. Yet, despite that, I enjoy being with a woman who's smart and pretty. She doesn't need to be the best cook. . . . But Irish food. Sorry, I couldn't live on it. And, besides, I can't picture Emma in the kitchen." Samuel could hear how muddled his words sounded, yet he kept going. "She and her cousin Bernadette plan to open a shop selling their lace goods. What's more, they're thinking about moving to an apartment building for women."

Sadie raised her eyebrows. Then she said, "She seems to be a very independent young woman. You could invite her to visit us here. She would see and experience more of our culture. I wonder if her aunt would permit Emma to take the train if she traveled with her cousin."

"Sadie, what a good idea. I'll write to invite her."

September 15, 1905
Dear Emma,
　　I enjoyed my short visit with you and listening to your music. Rajaa'an, thank your aunt Agnes for the lunch.
　　My buying trip in Pittsburgh was a success. I purchased some blue suspenders, fabric and patterns, besides the usual items we keep in our inventory.
　　It would be nice if you could visit me in New Salem. If Bernadette traveled with you, would it be permissible? You both could stay at the inn.
　　I look forward to your reply
Salaam,
Samuel

When the new goods arrived at the Uniontown train station, Anthony and Samuel packed them in the cart they drew behind the buggy. Traveling with the goods wouldn't be so easy once winter began. But on this fall day the sun beat down on them.

Their first stop was at the Benko farm outside the village of McClellandtown. On the way there, Anthony had told Samuel about the

Benkos. The family was large—seven girls and four boys—but no larger than many of the others. Mr. Benko, like other men in the area, worked in a mine but also farmed, joining his wife and children at the chores after coming home from the mine.

The farm sat at the top of a high hill. Lower hills and plenty of land surrounded it. The Benkos had a few cows and pigs, many chickens and turkeys, and a garden full of fall vegetables. When Samuel and Anthony drove up, the little ones stopped playing in the pumpkin patch and ran to the buggy.

The front door opened onto a wraparound porch. Mrs. Benko rushed out, smiling, to see what the peddlers had this time. "Oh, I love this blue cotton fabric! I'll make the boys shirts and dress them up with these blue suspenders. So much nicer than the drab brown ones they wear all the time." Then she spent a while going through the patterns, looking for one to make dresses for her girls.

Samuel organized her order—a pair of steel toe work boots, and the blue fabric and matching thread. Just as she was ready to pay, Mrs. Benko paused, deep in thought. Samuel watched and waited. "I'd love to have the light blue linen fabric to make myself a new dress," she finally said. "It's been so long since I've had a new one for church. But I think I may be short of cash."

"Don't worry. If you can't pay me, God will," Samuel told the woman.

"You're so kind. Bless you. Please wait here. I have some freshly picked vegetables for you." She came back a minute later with a bag of squash and potatoes. "Here you are. On your next visit, I'll settle my bill with you. If you're going on to Ronco, it's faster to take that path over there."

At one point during the shortcut through the Benkos' farmland, Anthony turned to Samuel. "We're both kind businessmen, and I approve of giving Mrs. Benko time to pay. But we do have to be careful with how often we make such a gesture to our customers."

"Father does this."

"Your father is a good-hearted and wise man. He knows when to say 'God will pay.' Yet it may not always work out. Your faith is talking. There will be times when you'll have to be tough enough to say 'no pay, no goods.'"

"I understand. It's odd. I worry about my savings, about being able to buy an automobile and have a family—and then my kindness wins out."

"Kindness is good, but we have to use it carefully in business deals. For me, honesty and trust come first."
Samuel looked at Anthony with an even greater sense of admiration.

7

___

John's carpenter shop to talk about making a Christmas gift for Tony. But there was a second motive: the letter in his pocket. They had become close enough friends that Samuel wanted John's advice. The two sat down on a bench outside the shop.

"You look so serious," John said. "Is something wrong?" Samuel pulled out the letter and read it aloud.

> *November 1, 1905*
> *Dear Saddo,*
>
> *I have read your letter many times. You sound well and happy with your work.*
>
> *Amina told me some of your news from your first letter home. I was visiting Aleppo with my family and went to see her. Her wedding celebration was a special time—all that dancing and singing. I miss seeing you and dream of coming to America. Of course, my parents will not allow me to travel there alone. And now they are worried about my future. Because of this, they have arranged for me to meet and marry the son of one of their friends.*
>
> *Your description of Independence Day makes me want to go to the free country.*
>
> *Life goes on here in Damascus, but not happily. The Young Turks are organizing for a revolution. They are protesting the higher taxes being imposed on Christians. I would like to go on to university to study languages and business, but my parents feel strongly that I must marry. What shall I do? Please write soon.*
> *Salaam,*
> *Zawhea*

"John, she'll marry, but it won't be to me. Even if we'd arranged our marriage before I left the country, I still don't have enough money to start a family. If it weren't for the political upheavals in Syria, her parents might not be in a rush to marry her."

"My friend, we can't do a thing about our beloved country but pray. You've only been here a few months, and you've had so much going on in your life. Maybe that's why your head is so confused. You told me you wrote to Emma after your visit, and now you talk as if you love Zawhea. Listen. I married only a few years ago. Yet I can tell you that love has a way of showing up just when the time is right."

"I don't know who I love. Emma hasn't written back to me. I left Syria thinking I might marry Zawhea someday. Now all I can do is write back to her and offer my support." He grew quiet. "Thanks for listening."

"You're my friend. I'm here whenever you want to talk."

"The letter wasn't the only reason I came. Can I use your shop to make Tony a wooden train for Christmas?"

"Of course. Come by any time. Let me grab you a key. Now, a glass of *arak* at the tavern?"

By the time Samuel got home from the tavern, he felt calm enough to write to Zawhea.

November 22, 1905
Dear Zawhea,

I received your letter. I am relieved to hear that you and your parents are well.

What a terrible situation in Syria now. And it seems to be getting worse. I am fearful for our country and pray for it every day. Your parents must be very worried about the future that they want to arrange a marriage for you right now. It is a difficult time, and I hesitate to advise you. In better times, you would be wise to continue your studies.

As for myself, I am working hard and saving so that someday I can marry and have a family. I often think what it would be like to have you here with me. I wish I could bring you here now.

Please write again.

Salaam,
Saddo

THE SYRIAN PEDDLER

8

During the winter months, the goods Samuel and Anthony bought and sold—heavy jackets, winter boots, hats, gloves—were heavier to transport. Since Arab and Coalie had to pull more weight, every trip took longer.

Because of the cold air outside, Samuel spent more time inside his customers' homes doing business. He came to realize that many of them were now his good friends too—due in part to the fact that he'd gotten better at speaking their native language. As time went on, he discovered more and more families that had emigrated from their country to work in the coal mines.

On an overcast December day, he stopped at the post office for the mail. A letter from his mother was waiting. When he got home, he read it in the quiet of his room.

December 5, 1905
Dear Samuel,

We love receiving your letters so full of news. We are smiling with happiness that you are doing well. And how nice that you took your father's name in America.

I am writing you about Zawhea. It seems that her parents arranged for her to meet a young man—a son of their friends. The last time I saw Zawhea and her family was at Amina's wedding. Those girls looked so lovely in their gowns. You remember that day and night, of course. I watched you and Zawhea dancing. You appeared to be fond of each other. Amina and Zawhea have seen each other often since the wedding. If you write your sister and ask about Zawhea's situation, she may be able to tell.

Rajaa'an, thank Anthony and Sadie for all they do for you We miss you. Your father sends his love.
Salaam,
Umm

THE SYRIAN PEDDLER

Samuel read the letter many times then folded it and put it away. He had sent several letters to his family, but Emma's name hadn't appeared in any of them. And why should it? After all, he'd seen her only once since June.

The idea of Zawhea getting married weighed on him. He picked up the replica of his church back home from the top of the chest. While he was turning it round and round, there was a loud knock on his door. "Can I come in?" It was Tony's voice. Samuel opened the door and looked down at his little friend, still bundled up in his jacket and hat and clutching a notebook.

Tony rushed past Samuel saying, "You should see my drawings" and jumped onto the bed. He noticed Samuel's face. "Are you sad? What's that you're holding?"

"It's my church back home. Well, a replica of it." "Replica? That means statue?" "A model."

"Are you sad because of that model?"

"No. Holding this model makes me feel better. I was a bit sad because I just read a letter from my family, and I miss them."

"I'm your family here in America. Right?"

Samuel couldn't help but smile. "Yes, you are, my little man. Now let's see those drawings."

"Here. Look. It's a train and a horse. I really want to go on a train ride and I really want a horse like Arab."

Samuel looked closely at the drawings. "You know, this train looks just like the one in Uniontown. And the horse does look like Arab. See if you can draw a picture of my church."

"I will as soon as I get a cookie."

Later that evening Samuel sat down and began to write.

December 15, 1905
Dear Zawhea,

We are about to celebrate the Feast of St. Nicholas. I am thinking about the many celebrations of this feast our families had together. One I remember in particular. You and I were in my umm's kitchen dishing out the malfouf, and I dropped a few of them on the floor. We laughed as you helped me clean up the sauce, rice, and meat slopped everywhere. I miss those happy times.

 I received a letter from Umm today. She mentioned that you had met the son of your parents' friends. I understand that if your parents want you to marry now, you will have no choice but to do so. Even here in America, some marriages are arranged and others are not, depending on the culture of those involved.

 I miss you. And I pray for our families and our country every day as Syria struggles against Ottoman control.

Salaam,

Saddo

Samuel folded the letter and addressed the envelope. Then he turned the bed-covers down and, after taming his agitated thoughts, fell asleep. But it wasn't a fitful sleep. In one of his dreams, he and Zawhea were in his mother's kitchen. Moments later, he was only an observer, seeing her standing stiffly next to a man he didn't recognize.

The next day, when he went to mail his letter to Zawhea, the postmaster gave him a letter, just a few lines, from Emma. She explained that Aunt Agnes wouldn't approve of her taking the train to visit Samuel even if Bernadette was along. *If you ask me, Aunt Agnes is too protective and strict,"* Emma wrote. *"I hope soon to move to the apartments for women, and then I can do as I please."* She ended the letter saying that the shop was busy, that she was grateful to Sadie for the invitation and, finally, that she missed him.

Samuel knew that by week's end he would have John read Emma's letter and ask for his advice. *My advice to myself? That Emma and I continue to write and to see each other when I'm on buying trips.* He let out a long sigh. *None of this helps to lessen the loneliness I feel here, at this moment.*

Samuel had always loved the Christmas season. For two reasons he especially welcomed it this year: He hoped it would distract him from his preoccupation over Zawhea and Emma, and he was curious to see what the season was like in a different country.

New Salem was preparing to celebrate the holiday. The shops were decorated in pine and red velvet ribbon, guests admired the decorated Christmas tree in the tavern, and the children were bubbling with excitement. He'd bought small gifts to ship to his family and for Anthony and Sadie. Tony would get the toy train Samuel had been making in his free time.

He was walking home early one evening after finishing the caboose, his hands in his pockets, softly singing one of his favorite songs, Ala DalOuna The homes and shops were lit with candles. The aromas of holiday foods managed to drift into the street despite the closed windows and doors. A great sense of peace came over him. *I think I'm finally beginning to feel at home here. The people are kind and have welcomed me—inviting me inside when I make deliveries, asking me to stay for dinner. Tomorrow, at the Feast of St. Nicholas, I'll pray for their health and I'll thank the Lord for my place here.*

Tony met Samuel at the door. "We saved you some dinner. I want to tell you about school," the boy said and followed Samuel to the kitchen.

When they were both seated, Samuel said, "Now, Tony, tell me the news." "I learned about St. Nicholas. He protects children and merchants—me

and you. And he leaves candy in our shoes."

"Yes, he's an important saint. Where are your shoes?" "Oh, I put them by the door."

Sadie walked in looking for Tony. "There you are. It's time for bed." "Do I have to go to bed right now?" Tony whined. "Yes. Tomorrow is the big feast day."

A short time later Samuel picked up his pen and paper to write his mother.

> *December 17, 1905*
> *Dear Umm,*
>
> *I have read your letter many times. You are right—I am fond of Zawhea. I am working hard and saving liras, but I cannot send for her now. Anthony has been kind to me, and we work well together. He will soon open his own store. Once that happens, I will take over the sale of goods to our customers. Then I will feel more secure about my ability to maintain a family.*
>
> *I have written to Zawhea. It is my desire that we stay in touch.*

LINDA HANNA LLOYD

I have been feeling the need to tell you about a young woman who is here in America. I met her, a fellow first-class passenger, during the crossing. Her name is Emma Monahan, and she is from Ireland. I had time to talk to passengers in the evening after dinner, and she is one of them I got to know. Emma is very pretty, but in a different way from Zawhea. She plays the piano. She also designs and makes lace—skills she learned from her mother. Someday she plans to open a lace shop with her cousin.

Anthony met Emma soon after she and I reached Manhattan. She lives in Brooklyn, a part of New York City, with her relatives. At Anthony's suggestion, and with his blessing, I went to visit her in September. It was during the same buying trip to Pittsburgh I mentioned to you that Anthony asked me to make. Before going to Pittsburgh, I traveled to New York City and stayed with George Nadar, a friend of the Abrahams, in a community known as Little Syria. His family welcomed me. George owns a dry goods store, which I visited. (It is exactly what I dream of for myself.) From George's home, I went to visit Emma. There, I was also welcomed. Her aunt had prepared lunch for me. The Irish are very different from us, even more than I expected. And when I thought about our customs and our religion, I knew that in my heart I am and will always be Syrian.

I now turn to other news. We decorated for the Christmas season with the St. Nicholas statue, pine boughs, and the Advent wreath. Tony is very excited and ready for small gifts tomorrow night, a few coins. I will think of you when I go to church this Saturday. Do you know that Father Raphael Hawaweeny arrived in New York City several years ago? Father Raphael travels around the country helping to organize Arabic-speaking parishes. He comes to New Salem only to perform baptisms and weddings. We have him to thank for blessing the parish created by the families here and for sending us a visiting priest for the holidays.

I sent you a package of small gifts. I hope you receive them in time for Christmas Day. My gift for little Tony is a wooden toy train, which I have almost finished making at my friend's carpenter shop. Tony is a joy, and being with him makes me long for a child of my own.

THE SYRIAN PEDDLER

I pray for your safety. (Of course, I am very concerned about our country's takeover by the Ottomans.) I think of you and Abb every day and miss you greatly.
Salaam,
Samuel

The next afternoon while Tony was outside playing, Anthony and Samuel sat at the kitchen table, enjoying a strong cup of *ahweh*. Sadie was cooking for the evening feast. Anthony began to play his oud, and Samuel, deeply moved by his native music, bent his head in prayer, and said softly, "*Inshallah* families will stay safe." God willing.

Anthony stopped playing in mid-song. He sat up, his back rigid, and then pounded his fist on the table. "The Christians aren't being accepted within the Ottoman Empire," he shouted. "Trust me. The Ottomans will drive our people out because of higher taxes and religious persecution."

To calm Anthony, Samuel reached across the table and took his hand. Sadie came over to join them. "I think about this every day," she said. "Let us pray together."

After a moment of silence, Samuel cleared his throat, got up, and paced. "I believe it's the possible takeover that is driving Zawhea's parents to want her married. Who knows what the future holds."

Anthony's eyes grew wide. "Samuel, you didn't tell us this latest news about Zawhea. I got the idea that you were fond of her. Is she really to be married?"

"Yes. *Umm* told me in her last letter," he replied, his voice faltering. "Zawhea's parents had arranged for her to meet a friend of their family." He covered his face. "Right now I can't afford to bring her here to marry me. What am I to do?"

"You're still young and have your dreams," Anthony said. "Keep working as hard as you're doing, and soon you'll have your own business. Then you'll be ready to start a family. Until then, you can continue to live with us."

"But what about Emma?" Sadie asked as she went back to cooking. "Do you have feelings for her? If so, take time to sort them out."

Samuel hesitated. "Yes, I have feelings for Emma. Yet she's so different from Zawhea in many ways. Her culture, her religion, her appearance, her goals. Our customs are strong, and that causes me to wonder if Emma's family would accept me. Emma wants to own her own shop and work as a

52

professional woman. Zawhea's parents want her to marry. . . . I have to think and pray about this."

Samuel looked toward Sadie, who was rinsing cabbage at the sink. He had come to respect her opinions, seeing her as the rock of the family. As Sadie wiped her hands and walked to the table, he watched her in anticipation.

"Samuel," she began gently, "have you written to Emma since you told me she wasn't allowed to visit us?"

He rubbed his forehead. "No. I've been too busy. But I do think about her."

Sadie smiled. "Thinking doesn't help. Let me tell you something about women. If a certain man likes us, we want to know by a gesture or a conversation. Emma may be wondering why you haven't written." She put a hand on his shoulder. "Try not to worry. Your life will follow God's plan. Continue to pray."

"What's wrong with me? Of course. I'll write Emma. After all, what can I do about Zawhea? Nothing." Samuel went to the counter, picked up a ball of meat, and rolled the cabbage around it. "You know, I love your *malfouf mahshi*."

9

The community celebrated the Feast that evening after church services, sharing mezza before they went on to their homes for the evening meal. The men played their ouds and darbukas while children, full of anticipation of St. Nick's visit, danced and played around the open area in the middle of the hall.

Tony stopped dancing. He ran over to Sadie and pulled at her dress. *Umm*, please can we go home so I can put my shoes outside for St. Nick? I'm sure he'll leave coins and candy."

"Son, we'll go soon."

Hearing this, Tony started to run toward the dancing. But first he went to pull on Samuel's shirt.

Samuel felt the tug and turned around. "Tony, you rascal. Say hello to Mr. Nazzif. We'll play later at home."

Tony looked up at John. "Hello, sir," he said timidly.

John bent down and placed a hand on the boy's shoulder. "I'm happy to meet you. I'm your friend Margaret's father."

Tony shook his head and ran back to his friends.

"The children are such fun to watch," John said. "Look at Tony with his dress shirt and suspenders, tie flying in the air as he tries to dance with the older children. I've been watching Margaret follow him around. My little girl is growing up quickly. . . . By the way, her dress was made from the linen you sold my wife. Elena is an excellent seamstress. She even designs dresses without a pattern."

It was still snowing as they left the church. Samuel threw a few snowballs at Tony. The boy was quick to scoop up handfuls and shower Samuel with snowflakes.

After the Feast of St. Nicholas, it seemed that Christmas would be there in no time. Samuel was happy he'd finished Tony's gift. Now there was time to fine-tune the new business plan he and Anthony had begun last week

Their customers had doubled in number, and Anthony was seriously thinking about opening his own shop so some of them could come to him. They would still peddle to the communities of miners, and Samuel would take on some of the customers as his own.

After he finished the plan, he wrote to Emma.

> *December 19, 1905*
> *Dear Emma,*
>> *Work has been very busy with Christmas approaching. We have many orders to fill. Are you keeping up with the holiday orders for your lace?*
>> *I am sorry you cannot visit New Salem. I would like you to meet my friends and see my town. It is especially festive now.*
>> *I hope to visit you on my next buying trip.*
> *Merry Christmas,*
> *Samuel*

On Christmas Eve, the families of St. George Parish gathered around an unlit bonfire outside their church. They all held lighted candles, and one of the children read the Christmas story aloud. Then the priest lit the bonfire as the parishioners sang psalms, preparing for the birth of the Christ Child.

Early on Christmas morning Samuel was awakened by Tony's shouts from the staircase. " *Umm, Abb*, Samuel. Papa Noel has come." Hearing Tony, everyone got up to see him by the tree, looking at all the gifts. His eyes were as bright as the church candles when Samuel gave him the train. He closely eyed the small black chunks of wood that Samuel had made to look like coal.

"Oh, *Umm!*" Tony exclaimed. "A train with an engine, a caboose and two coal cars carrying real coal!"

"It's wonderful, son," Sadie said. "You should know that Samuel made that for you in John Nazzif's carpenter shop."

Tony turned to Samuel. "I think you have to be very smart to make a train. Can we go to Uniontown soon to see the real one?"

With pure joy, Samuel watched Tony play with the train and his other new toys. *It takes so very little to bring happiness to children.*

10

It had been almost a year since Samuel first ventured onto the pavement of Manhattan. He had stopped worrying about being discriminated against for his dark skin. The people of New Salem and the nearby communities accepted the Syrian immigrants, just as they did the Polish, Slavs, and Italians. This spring day he was going to purchase a horse and cart at the livery stable on Center Street. He was in a cheery mood, excited about having his own transportation—even though he was in the middle of a serious discussion with Anthony, who had come along to advise him.

Samuel had heard again from his family that the Ottomans were taking over the country and driving the Christians out. He was worried about them and about Zawhea. "What do you think?" he asked Anthony. "With the takeover and the taxation issue making things so difficult at home, should we bring our families over?"

"In the last letter I received, my family said they wanted to stay in Syria or else travel to France. America wasn't mentioned. My feeling is that your family wants the same. Do you want to go back to visit?"

Samuel pulled the reins to slow down Arab and Coalie. He bit his lower lip before replying. "To travel there now isn't within reason." His voice was wistful. "Our business won't allow such a long journey. I think if I did go back, my parents would be disappointed in me. They want me to have a good life here. Perhaps one day they'll join me." By this point, his voice was shaky.

After regaining his composure, he hitched up the horses at the livery stable. Since it was close to the other shops, Sadie had given the men a list of goods to buy from the grocer. But first they would look over the horses.

Samuel often stopped at the stable on his travels to the coal communities and he'd had his eye on a certain horse that reminded him of Arab. He felt he had a way with Arab and wanted a horse just like him. He called to Anthony, "Over here. This may be the one." The horse was as black as morning coffee and had a shiny mane. When Samuel looked him in the eyes the horse looked into Samuel's, as if they were talking to each other, just like Arab did.

Anthony examined the animal. "It's a fine one, but a little short and stocky. Listen. I've been thinking of buying a horse for Tony since he'll be able to help with deliveries in the coming year. You and Arab have such a connection to each other. Would you accept Arab for your own?"

Samuel shook his head in disbelief. "You're too generous. No. I'll pay you for Arab. He's a wonderful horse. And this stocky one may be just right for Tony." He smiled. "I can see Tony's face now when you tell him he's going to have his very own horse."

"He'll be one happy boy. Then it's a deal. I'd like to bring Tony here to see this horse first. Maybe on Saturday. But for now, let's finish the errands." Anthony and Samuel always took their time when shopping was involved. All the merchants were good friends, so they stayed to talk about the news in the town, or their families in the old country. That day the most important topic was the West Penn Trolley Line: Its route was extending to New Salem and Masontown.

"Anthony, you know what this means," said Samuel. "Our customers will be able to come to us and shop."

"What good news—and just in time for our new spring inventory."

One day in early May, Samuel started to prepare for another buying trip to Pittsburgh. He was thinking about seeing Emma. He felt bad that he hadn't written her more often. He paused at his task and scratched his head, wondering about the men who often stayed at the hotel. *Is she fond of one of them? Maybe one of them has shown an interest in her piano playing.*

That evening he arrived home to find a letter from Zawhea.

April 5, 1906
Dear Saddo,

I am sorry I have not written you sooner. I am now married to Abraham Nader. The wedding took place in January. You know how much I wanted to attend university, but I really had no choice in the matter. (You are well aware of what Syrian parents can be like when it is time for a daughter to marry.) Abraham is a member of the Committee of Union and Progress. These men are working to free us from Ottoman control. The work is dangerous and I do not understand why he cannot work in trade. However, the one piece of good news is that we are living in Aleppo, where I may be able to pursue my studies.

I see Amina often. Her friendship means much to me.
I miss you as a friend, and I pray for you every day.
Salaam,
Zawhea

With the letter in hand, going down the stairs two at a time, he shouted to anyone who was listening, "She's married."

Sadie came from the kitchen to the bottom of the stairs. She stood there, hands on her hips, gazing at him in surprise. "Samuel, what are you talking about?"

"Zawhea writes that she's married and lives in Aleppo. I knew this would happen."

Sadie led him to the kitchen, where eggplants and onions on the table were waiting to be chopped. "Samuel, you're like a brother to me. A brother who sounds confused about love. Time will show you the way to your future life as a husband and a father. I watch you with Tony, and I know beyond a doubt that you'll be a wonderful father." She gestured toward the chairs. "Please sit with me. I tire easily now."

Samuel looked at her in confusion.

"I'm going to have a baby in November. We've been dreaming about another child for a long time. . . . Tony doesn't know, but we'll tell him soon."

At that moment, Samuel's troubles disappeared. He gave Sadie a hug. "I'm so happy for you and Anthony. And Tony will love having a new brother or sister."

"We'll see. He's been an only child for six years. So it may be difficult for him to share us with a little one."

After dinner that evening, Samuel was in the living room reading the newspaper when Tony skipped in to join him. He expected Tony to describe every detail about going to the livery stable with his *abb* to get his new horse. So the boy's words took him by surprise.

Umm has a baby in her tummy," Tony said. "It may be a little sister. It may be a little brother. Either way, I'll be a big brother." His smile faded. "Will you still be my big brother?"

"I'll always be like your big brother," Samuel replied. "And you're going to be the best big brother ever." He picked Tony up and sat him on his lap. "I have something to tell you. You know your *abb* and *umm* will need a bedroom for the baby. So I'll be moving soon."

Tony looked stricken. "Will you go far away?"

"Not far away. I'll be in another house in New Salem. You can come visit me anytime. We'll go riding with our horses. By the way, did you name your horse yet?"

"I've been thinking about that. Can I name him Sammy?"

"Good thinking. A horse named after me. I like that." He hugged the boy then said, "Quick, now. Go get ready for bed. It's late, and you're a growing boy who needs plenty of rest."

11

June 20, 1906
Dear Emma
    I will be on another buying trip in August. I hope it is possible to see you once again. I plan to be in New York City on August 29.
    Your letters are arriving more quickly than before, now that the train station has opened in Uniontown. Please write to let me know if that date is agreeable for you.
    Business is going well—so well that Anthony will soon open his own store.
Salaam,
Samuel

July 20, 1906
Dear Samuel,
    I will be waiting for you on August 29. Come to the hotel around the dinner hour. I will be playing then. Afterward we can have dinner together.
Fondly,
Emma

Walking up to the hotel, Samuel noticed a parked automobile. He stopped to admire the two-seater Ford Model F. Its leather roof was rolled back. He straightened his tie, pushed his hat down over his forehead, and sauntered around the car—even checking the wheels as if he were an expert. *Someday this will be mine.*

He tipped his hat as the owner approached the vehicle. "Good afternoon, sir. What a grand Model F you have. Are you satisfied with its performance?"

"It's a dream. A good runabout with two forward speeds and a reverse," the man replied. "My young man, save your money and you'll own one too."

Samuel went into the café feeling jaunty. Several men were watching Emma at the piano playing "On a Sunday Afternoon." Many of the guests sang along:

"In the merry month of June,
Take a trip on the Hudson or down the bay,
Take a trolley to Coney or Rockaway,
On a Sunday afternoon,
You can see the lovers spoon.
They work hard on Monday,
But one day that's fun day
Is Sunday afternoon."

It was as if Samuel didn't know her. She was stunning in a sapphire-blue silk evening gown with a low, lacy bodice. As she bent over the piano keys, the top of her bosom could be seen, leaving the men wanting more. Samuel could picture her tightening a pink corset, bending down to pull up sheer stockings, and finally stepping into lacy drawers and a petticoat. *Seduction couldn't be easy with so many layers of clothing. . . . What am I thinking?*

Finishing the last piece, she looked up and took in the applause. She spotted Samuel. Her eyes shining, she stood up and walked toward him. It had been close to a year since they last saw each other.

He shook her hand, aware of the people around them. "Emma, your piano music is as beautiful to my ears as you are to my eyes. You really seem to enjoy entertaining the guests."

Emma blushed. "I do. I do very much. Oh, Samuel. How wonderful to see you again. Shall we get a table for dinner? I want to hear all about you and how your business is going."

During dinner, halfway through his tales of customers and friends he had a brilliant idea. "The lace on your gown is lovely. I assume it's something you designed and made."

Emma nodded.

"What would you think about Anthony and me selling your lace? We could purchase an agreed-upon number of pieces from you."

"The women there will love our lace. We have several designs of lace collars. What a grand idea. Come by the shop in the morning. We have a good selection for you to see, and we can discuss the details. I'm sure Bernadette will agree to this." She put down her knife and fork. "Now, how about some fun this evening after we've finished eating? Bernadette and I are going to the church hall dance. Would you come with us?"

Samuel thoughtfully rubbed his chin. Finally he replied, but with hesitation, "Yes, I'll come. But know that most of my dancing has been the *dabke* at our celebrations at home. You'll have to teach me your Irish dances."

"If your *dabke* is a folk dance, then it's probably similar to our Irish quadrille. Don't worry. You'll learn quickly."

Emma and Samuel were a very attractive couple on the dance floor that evening. She laughed as he whirled her around, her dress billowing with each twirl. He'd rolled up his shirtsleeves and removed his tie against the heat. It brought him joy to see people from young to very old dancing together, the same as dances were in Syria.

During the first break, Samuel met many of Emma's friends and the friends of her aunt and uncle. While Emma carried on conversations, he looked around the hall. He was the only one there who looked Mediterranean.

This didn't bother him at all until two fiddlers, during a later break, sat down close to where he and Emma were catching their breath.

"Where are you from?" asked the shorter of the two. "We never see people with black skin in our church. Are you even allowed here?" Emma's face turned red with anger. "Samuel is my friend, and of course he's allowed here," she said as loud as she could without attracting attention. "Don't be so prejudiced."

Samuel did his best to control himself. "Sir, I'm a Syrian Christian. I live near Pittsburgh and have a successful business. The men in Syria all have dark olive skin—we are not black." He turned to Emma. "Let's go outside and get some fresh air."

They walked out the side door of the hall to a grassy area. He pointed to one of the benches off to the side. "Let's sit. I need to think about what just happened—as well as what Mario told me in the kitchen of the *Neustria* I've been called black more than I like, but at least now I'm able to control my temper."

"Samuel, this is why my family settled in an Irish community when they arrived in America. And it's why the community of Little Syria exists. Immigrants tend to settle among others of their own culture." Then she said softly, "Your skin color doesn't bother me."

"I know that. Maybe I'm in a dream world thinking I'll be accepted everywhere in this great country." He gave her a gentle hug and lightly kissed both her cheeks.

Emma didn't pull away. Instead, she murmured, "Let's find a place where we won't be seen. Over there. Behind that clump of trees."

Just as they sat down on the grass, Bernadette called from the door of the hall, "Emma? Samuel? Are you out here? The dancing has started again."

Emma's hand froze on Samuel's cheek. She took a deep breath before replying. "Yes, we'll be back in soon, Bernadette. The fresh air feels good."

He helped her up, and they tiptoed from the trees toward the road behind them. "Word will surely get out about this, and at some point we'll hear about it," she told him.

Samuel hummed tunes from last night's dance as he strode into the hotel the next morning. He entered the shop and paused to gaze at the white and ecru lace collars and pendants in many different designs. The display convinced him of Emma's and Bernadette's talents. When he'd been there last September, they sold only to tailors. Now they were selling their goods in the hotel shop. News of their lace had spread by word of mouth. Guests, relatives, and locals had become their customers, and Samuel was about to join the group. He had a good feeling that the women and girls in and around New Salem would enjoy wearing the lace with their finest dresses.

He'd come to the shop so Emma could help him select the designs. Her aunt and Bernadette were also there. The air grew thick with comments and opinions. After a while, Samuel was uncomfortably aware of the wall clock's ticking: He had a train to catch.

After some debate, Samuel chose a dozen collars and six lace pendants. What they did agree on quickly was that Samuel would pay the purchase price for the collars and pendants and sell them at a profit. When he needed more, he would order them by telegram. After hurried goodbyes, he dashed out of the shop.

Later, on the train, he had time to think about last night. He wondered if Emma had been quizzed on their whereabouts when Bernadette came looking for them. *Life surely is interesting. And it can be very complicated. Emma's aunt means well. Yet she was nosy this morning about my religion. Did she think I was going to ask for Emma's hand in marriage? Then again, she'd been in the dance hall, and who knows what she saw or thought. . . . Or maybe it's the color of my skin . . .*

12

Two events were fast approaching: Sadie's due date and Thanksgiving. Samuel's anticipation of both had been slightly marred by his search for lodging. Many people who owned houses took in boarders for extra income, and he'd looked at several rooms. But he preferred to find a small home and have his privacy.

Just when he was about to give up, his friend John told him about a place in town. It was perfect—a bedroom, parlor, and kitchen with a coal-burning stove. The grocer's son and his wife lived on the other side.

On a cold November afternoon that threatened rain, John helped Samuel move. Anthony and Tony joined them. There wasn't much to move. Samuel had bought a kitchen table and two chairs and built his own chest of drawers in John's carpenter shop. He'd ordered a mattress from the Pittsburgh Mercantile Company, upon John's recommendation, which, at least for now, would go on the floor. The bed frame he would buy later, after saving more money. Sadie and Anthony had given him a couch that was sitting, unused, in their basement. The women from the church were happy to give him dishes and other extras to start a home, some of them seemingly new. Aside from this, there were clothes, books, gas lamps, and a few other items he'd collected during his first year in America. The business inventory would remain in Anthony's barn.

In a few hours, Samuel was looking over his new living quarters. He felt quite proud. He thanked Anthony, Tony, and John and then paused. "Wait. Before you leave, I have something for each of you." He pulled three books out of a bag. "For you, Tony, a book about a bunny named Benjamin. I know you'll smile your way through the story. And for you men, *The Adventures of Tom Sawyer*. Mark Twain, the famous American author, wrote it. When I was in New York, I learned that he was one of the first guests at the Hotel Wolcott. The shop in the hotel sells his books."

Tony gave Samuel a big hug. "Will you come over to help me read my new book?"

Anthony answered for Samuel. "Of course he will. But later. Right now we have to go home to Mother. She needs our help getting ready for the baby."

Samuel told Tony, after he was bundled up in his coat, cap, and gloves, "I'll visit you soon to read your new book."

Once Tony and Anthony were out the door, Samuel turned to John. "I owe you a glass of *arak* Several of them. Let's go to the tavern."

On the way, John said, "Let's take a minute and go to my shop. I have something to show you."

Samuel followed John into the workroom. "It's beautiful," he said, motioning to a bed frame. He got closer to examine it. "Finely crafted. Do you plan to start selling them?"

John burst into a belly laugh. "No, no. I made this as a gift for you. So you don't have to sleep on the floor."

Sam scratched his head in wonderment. "What a surprise. You're a kind and a good friend. And an excellent craftsman. Now let me buy you that drink."

The two slapped each other on the back and headed to the tavern. Inside, the atmosphere was jovial on this Saturday evening, due in part to the coming holidays, and even more so to the general sense that the economy was thriving.

Samuel settled comfortably into his own space. During the day, he made calls on customers. In the evenings, he read Mark Twain, gave thought to his business, and wrote letters to his family and Emma. The holidays would be here soon, and the news was spreading about his perfect Christmas gifts— lace collars and pendants. Anthony was quite happy about this. He viewed the items as perfect additions to the store he would open next spring.

One morning Samuel left a farm, having finished an early call there, and headed for town. He and Anthony had arranged to meet on Main Street. When he passed the Benko farm, he smiled over the goings-on in that household. One of the daughters was to be married soon. *One daughter fewer for Mrs. Benko to "encourage" me about.*

Samuel heard little Tom Benko call out, "Mr. Hanna! Stop!"

He pulled on the reins and waited for the boy to reach him. "My mother sent me with a message," he said, panting. "Please come right away. She's in a fright over my sister's wedding dress."

Samuel looked down at the thin boy. "But what's wrong, Tom?"

"She doesn't have enough fabric. And a needle broke on the machine."

"Then let's go see what we can do for her."

The boy hopped up on the buggy and rode to the house with Samuel. Mrs. Benko was waiting on the front porch. "Oh, Samuel," she cried, leading him inside. "Thank you for stopping. I know you're a busy man." "Mrs. Benko, how can I help you today? Tom said you're working on a wedding dress." He glanced at the woman's sewing machine, the first Singer in the area.

She held up the dress, made of organza and silk. "I'm in the midst of finishing the bodice, and I've run out of the silk fabric. And to make matters worse, the needle broke on my machine and I don't have an extra. You have others, don't you? Please say you do."

"I know we have more needles. And we may have some silk. I'll have to check when I'm in town." He looked at the dress more closely. "Have you seen my lace collars? I was saving them to sell as Christmas gifts. But one would be lovely on this. I'll bring a few back with me—just to see if you're interested. Can you wait until tomorrow?"

The furrows in the woman's forehead suddenly looked deeper. "The wed-ding is next month. Which sounds far off, but it's not."

"Then I'll come out later this afternoon. But it'll be much later."

"My dear man, God bless you. Come at dinnertime and you can eat with us. I hear you're living on your own now. So a home-cooked meal will be good for you."

Samuel smiled. "Word travels around, doesn't it?" He moved toward the door. "I'm on my way to meet Anthony in town. We're going to look at property for the new store. I'll see you this evening."

When Samuel reached Main Street, Arab began prancing around. Samuel looked down and realized the horse was trying to avoid broken glass. He heard angry voices coming from men standing in front of the grocer's market, their guns poised. When Samuel got closer, he could hear what they were saying.

"We got rid of the Cooley gang a few years ago." "Who is it now?" "Some varmints who learned from the old gang." "We'll hunt them down."

Sheriff Dan was attempting to calm the men. "We'll use all our powers to capture and penalize the culprits. For now, you can put down your arms.

Keep them handy, and use them only to protect your property or family. The constable and I are going to put together a posse to begin the search."

Samuel's heart was beating louder than the men's shouts. He took off to find Anthony.

Minutes later he was tying Arab up at the barn. He turned around and saw the door open. The bolt and locks were on the ground. Anthony was there, sweeping up glass from a broken window.

"Oh, no! They got us too!" Samuel ran into the barn then to the shelf where they kept the lace. It was empty. Shreds of fabric were scattered about where pieces had been ripped from the bolts. He kicked at them, running his hands through his hair and shouting, "The lace. The fabric. Anthony, you never prepared me for this. This wouldn't have happened at home. Do you realize how much of my savings I'll have to use to replace our losses?"

Anthony came into the barn and put his arm around Samuel. "I know. And I'm sorry. From what I've seen so far, they got away with fabric, clothing, and the lace. Whatever was light enough to carry off. Thankfully, we had our money secured in the house and bank. At least they didn't rob either of those places. And at least no one was injured."

Samuel pushed him away. "How can you be so calm? I've been saving for an automobile. And for my future. What will I do? God help me." He remembered the wedding dress and his promise. "Mrs. Benko. She needs needles for her Singer. And more fabric for her daughter's wedding dress. I told her I'd be back with them at dinnertime. The woman was desperate. . . There's nothing for me to do here. If I leave now, I can be in Uniontown to catch the next train to Pittsburgh. And I'll telegraph Emma to send more lace right away."

Anthony put up his hand. "Before you rush off to buy fabric in Pittsburgh, calm down so we can talk about a reasonable way to handle the problem."

"Calm down? That's easy for *you* to say. You haven't lost your savings. I had very little to begin with. . . . You don't understand."

"Yes, I do. I was in your same situation just a few years ago. Think Samuel. You still have money in the bank. Yes, we'll both need to pay for the new orders, and that will set both of us back. But you've never been a quitter. Or an angry man." He took a deep breath. "Look. Instead of you rushing off to Pittsburgh, we can telegraph Saehan. The trains have added more stops to their daily schedules. So we can have the replacements in a few days." He picked up the broom he had set down. "Now. I have to go to the house. I ordered Sadie and Tony to stay inside to be safe."

Samuel felt even more desolate. He hadn't even asked about the safety of those two people he loved. "My apologies, Anthony. For everything. I respect your calm-headed thinking. Yes, see to your family. I'll go to the Western Union in Uniontown. When I'm back, I'll go to Mrs. Benko's."

After Anthony had gone, Samuel paced back and forth in the barn, fighting back tears, thinking about the money he'd lost.

Two telegrams were on their way in a matter of a few hours.

Saehan Abraham, November 15 1906
Abraham's Wholesale, 900 Fifth Avenue Uptown,
Pittsburgh
Pennsylvania
We were robbed STOP Money sent C.O.D. STOP
Immediately replace our last fabric order. STOP
Samuel Hanna

Emma Monahan, November 15 1906
Hotel Wolcott, West Thirty-First Street, New York
City
Lace was stolen STOP Send replacements of original
purchase STOP Money to be sent C.O.D. STOP
Samuel Hanna

On the way to the Benko farm, Samuel thought about his losses. *Who knows how much of my savings I'll have to use to replace all the goods. This isn't fair. Whoever committed the crimes should suffer. I'm going to join the posse.*

When he walked up to the farmhouse, Mr. Benko was sitting on the porch, wearing a heavy coat and mumbling to himself. He held up his glass. "Hello, Samuel. Care for some *arak*?"

"No, thank you."

"Did you hear about the robberies? The sheriff came by the mine to talk to us just before we closed down. Said he'll meet with us tomorrow. My men are worried about their families and homes. Of course, the company store's been secured for the night."

Before Samuel could reply, Mrs. Benko joined them. "Are you okay? And the Abrahams?"

"Everyone is fine. But I have bad news. The thieves stole some of our inventory. We think only fabric and lace. I just sent telegrams. We'll have what you need in a few days." He pulled a small package from a pocket. "Here are more needles." "Jesus, Mary, and Joseph. Mr. Benko told me about the grocer's place. I've been in the kitchen praying no one else was robbed." With tears streaming down her face, she hugged Samuel. "Just take care of your business for now. I'll be praying for you and the others. The Good Lord will take care of us all. I'm also going to say a prayer for that fabric to get here in time. That dress is going to age me before all is said and done." She stopped inside the door and turned around. "I almost forgot. You were going to eat dinner with us."

"Maybe another evening, if you don't mind. I wouldn't be very good company right now."

"Then, soon," she said and went into the house.

Mr. Benko stood and put his hands on Samuel's shoulders. "I'm so sorry those good-for-nothings robbed you and Anthony. You're both hard-working men, and you don't deserve it. Believe me, we'll run those gangsters down and then run them out of here. Try not to get too stewed up over this."

"I can't help it. We've all worked hard, I know. But half my savings is gone."

With long faces, Anthony and Samuel began the inventory. They needed to account for missing items and total up their losses. A few minutes into the task, Samuel said, "Tell me more about the Cooley Gang."

"They were a fearless bunch. Jack and Frank Cooley—they were brothers—led the outlaws. For ten years, they robbed Fayette County farmers. Livestock. Savings. Anything else they could get their hands on. Each time, they'd escape by hiding in caves or crossing the border into West Virginia."

"Did anyone in the towns ever see them?"

"Plenty of times. But somehow, they always got away. It was said that on Sunday afternoons they'd show up at the Cooley homestead, brandishing their rifles. Their father always protected his boys. It was hard to capture them in the act of stealing. And the sheriffs were none too competent in catching them."

"How did it finally end?"

"One day word got out that they planned to rob the paymaster of Wynn Coke Works. They were going to attack him when he came from the bank with the payroll. Well, there happened to be a United States Secret Service detective in the county who was tracking down moonshiners. He joined the sheriff and the town posse trying to bring down the gang. During the so-called arrests, Jack and Frank Cooley were shot to death. The rest of the men were brought to trial and convicted. That was at least five years ago."

"Quite a story. Now I see why you have a rifle. But have there been many robberies since?"

"Some small petty thefts. But everyone is very careful about banking cash, securing inventories." Anthony paused. Samuel looked up. He'd never seen anyone look so remorseful. "Samuel," Anthony continued, "I should have told you about this a long time ago. But I didn't want you to worry. You were trying to settle into a new life. A new trade. A new country. You're right to be angry." His voice grew softer. "But anger won't help us get back to work." "I understand. . . . I also understand that I'm going to need more than my pocketknife for protection."

Tony sat beside Samuel as they rode to the Benko farm. When he wasn't in school, the boy, in small ways, had been helping Samuel with the business. Samuel had taken it upon himself to manage Anthony's customers as well as his own, since the baby's arrival was so close.

"Did they catch the robbers?" Tony asked.

"No. It's as if they disappeared into thin air," replied Samuel. "I think they've gone on to another town."

"I hope they're gone. I was scared. I can't wait for Thanksgiving. And then Christmas comes right behind it."

Samuel smiled at the boy's priorities. Then he thought about the two holidays. He and Anthony had felt so fortunate: The replacements for the stolen goods had arrived before Thanksgiving. That was why he and Tony were on their way to Mrs. Benko—to bring fabric and one of Emma's lace collars.

Samuel glanced at Tony, who was absorbed in the passing scenery. His own thoughts turned to Emma. *I wonder what's going on with her. She mailed me the lace pieces. But not a single word was included with the package.*

A beaming Mrs. Benko opened the door to Samuel and Tony. "I knew God would take care of us," she said and blessed herself.

"I'm just thankful the fabric arrived in time for you to finish the dress," said Samuel. "After all, it's one of the biggest days in your daughter's life."

"Esther will be so relieved. She's been worrying herself sick. Did you bring the lace collar too?"

He held it up. "Yes. Look at the delicacy of it. I also brought a pendant, in case you're interested. They're hand-crocheted. From the finest Irish cotton." "This collar is just the right finishing touch. Can I keep the pendant to show Esther? She won't be home until dinner."

"Of course you may. Take your time."

"Thank you. Remember now, I want to see you at the wedding." She leaned down to tell Tony, "Have some cookies." She pointed to a plate on the table. "And tell Samuel to eat some too. He needs more flesh on those bones." On the way home, Tony looked up at Samuel. "I think you should find a girl to dance with at the wedding. Don't you get lonesome without me around all the time?"

Samuel laughed. "Now that you ask, I do get lonesome."

13

December 1, 1906
Dear Samuel,

I have been thinking of you. You must be sad and angry about the crimes and your losses that you wrote me about. I pray that your community is safe, and I hope there have been no more robberies so you can thoroughly enjoy the Christmas season.

Everyone here is in a festive mood. We have decorated the hotel lobby and stairs with fresh greens and red bows. You can imagine how it looks with the stained-glass window and the velvet chairs. The guests are in good spirits. Many of them shop for gifts in our boutique. Bernadette and I are working hard to keep up with the holiday orders for lace, yours included. I can picture the women in New Salem wearing our lace collars. My heart is filled with happiness knowing you have been successful selling them. You and I have established a good business partnership that both Bernadette and I want to continue.

I have to tell you that I met an Irish man who stays at the hotel on business. We have become close, since he travels to the city often. I am still not sure of the direction of our relationship, yet we do share the same culture. He lives in Altoona, also located in Pennsylvania. That would be a dramatic change for me since I love the city.

I am very fond of you, Samuel. Because of this, the differences between our two cultures sadden me—as does the fact that we are not of the same religion. You know that I can never leave the Catholic faith.

Please forgive me if I have hurt you. You were such a dear companion on our adventure to America. I believe we were there for each other to keep our spirits up. I pray that we can continue our friendship. I will never forget you.

THE SYRIAN PEDDLER

Fondly,
Emma

Samuel read the letter for the tenth time. Then he gathered his jacket, hat, and gloves and slammed the door. He walked down the street, no destination in mind, packing the snow in balls and throwing them to the ground. *I should have written and visited her more. Now she sends me this letter just when I thought we were closer. At dinner with the Nadars, she didn't know how to eat our bread. And that sterile Irish living room at her aunt's—there wasn't a bit of warmth or color in it. Our relationship wouldn't have worked anyway. . . . Now Zawhea is married. Maybe this is God's way of giving me time to make the right choices.*

He ended up at John's home. After a cup of coffee and conversation, he walked back home in a calmer mood.

December 10, 1906
Dear Emma,
I received your letter. It was not easy to read. Yet you are right. We are not only from different countries but, more importantly, from different religions and traditions. That and the distance between us are hard to overcome. My life is here now, in New Salem, with my work and the dream of opening a store of my own.
I do want to continue both our friendship and our business partnership. I will never forget your beauty, your kindness, and the wonderful music you play.
Merry Christmas,
Samuel

From the time Samuel sent his letter to Emma, he stayed upset and angry. He welcomed the distractions of Christmas gift orders and holiday festivities.

One morning he left his house to buy gifts for Tony and his baby sister Rima. On the way, he compared last Christmas, when he'd made a train for Tony, to this one. Now he had so much less. It had been a tough time due to the robberies and loss of money.

At the market, he bought a book for Tony. For Rima he chose a teddy bear, a popular toy since President Teddy Roosevelt had taken office.

As soon as he left the store, the anger and sadness returned. He walked toward the grocer's, his head down, kicking at the snow beneath his feet.

"Whoa, my friend," John Nazzif said. "You almost walked right into me. What's bothering you?"

"Sorry, John. Emma writes that she's met another man. I can't believe it. First Zawhea and now her. . . . So what did our kisses mean?"

"This turn of events calls for a serious talk." They headed for the tavern.

"What is it with women?" Samuel asked as soon as they were seated.

"I didn't think I could be so angry with Emma. I was sure we'd be able to work out our differences." Samuel downed his glass of *arak*. "Her skin was so lovely to touch. I saw men yearning for her while she played the piano. It has to be one of them. And he probably has an automobile. Look at me. With only a horse." He slammed his fist on the table. "I'm going to buy a Model F just like the one I saw in front of her family's hotel. Did you know they get up to twenty-eight miles an hour? Just think how much faster I could make my rounds to customers. And that means more money in a day's work."

John laughed. "You're upset with Emma, and you're talking about an auto. You're one angry, determined man today." He grew serious. "You know, a woman and her family once shunned me. They didn't think I was good enough. That hurt my pride, and I handled it with anger. Now I have Elena and Margaret, and I wouldn't have my life any other way. We talked about this when you received the letter from Zawhea. I'm confused. Is it a wife you're wanting, or an auto?"

Samuel stood up. "Another glass?"

John shook his head. Then he leaned back, his arms crossed, and watched his friend go to the bar and return.

Samuel started in again. "I do want my own automobile, and now there's no woman in my life. . . . My father once told me something: Putting a motor car in order is child's play compared with getting a sick horse well. He read that in *The World's Work*. Arab is in good shape now. But who knows what the future holds?"

"I understand. Look. The Benko wedding is approaching. Come with Elena and me to the wedding. I know several young women who would enjoy a dance with you."

Samuel started to get up to buy a third drink. John gently pushed him back into his seat and said, "You'd be staggering home."

Samuel took a few deep breaths. "You're right. It's time for black coffee. Once again, you've offered good advice—and not just about forgoing another drink. Yes, I'll join you at the wedding and have a good time."

St. Thomas Catholic Church was new, built in Footedale to serve the Italian, Polish, and Slovak families of New Salem and the nearby communities. Before its doors opened, Catholics had to walk to Uniontown for church. The trek was long and hard, especially for the younger children. So the families pulled together and asked the bishop for help in building a church. The first wedding at St. Thomas was Esther Benko's on December 15.

Samuel made sure he arrived with time to spare. The pews, decorated with pine boughs and red velvet ribbons, had begun to fill with people speaking softly in anticipation. He was friends of both the bride and the groom, but he chose a seat, next to the aisle, on the side for the bride's family. After all, the wedding dress was almost "his."

Leaning over, he beamed when Esther passed by on the arm of her father. He couldn't stop gazing at the dress. It flowed in a tier from the waist to the floor, with a full organza bustle in the back. The lace collar was sewn on the scooping neckline of the fitted, silk bodice. *To think that I sold her the pattern, the fabric, and the lace.* Samuel knew Mrs. Benko was a good seamstress but this dress could have been designed and made in France.

After the ceremony, guests mingled outside the church. Snow flurries began to fall.

Passing slowly through the crowd, Samuel overheard comments. "Did you see the lace collar on her gown?" "I heard that Samuel Hanna sells those collars. And the lace pendant Mary Benko is wearing, he sells them too." "Good Christmas gifts." "That Mary Benko is a first-rate seamstress. She made Esther's dress." "Oh, the groom is so handsome. Do you know him?" "He's from Masontown and works for the Uniontown Hotel. A lovely couple."

When Anthony and Sadie joined Samuel outside, they'd heard some of the comments too. "The women are right," Sadie whispered to Samuel. "Esther's dress is gorgeous. And you made a smart move having one of your lace collars and pendants on display."

"I'm happy to see Esther look so beautiful," said Samuel. Rima started to whimper. "Could I hold her for you?" he asked. He took the baby in his arms, watching her closely and holding her tightly.

Tony pulled on his jacket. "Who are you going to dance with? There are girls here for the party."

"You can pick one out for me when the dancing begins," Samuel replied. Tony grinned and looked at his parents. They both smiled at him, shaking their head. Anthony asked his son, "Are you helping Samuel find a lady friend?"

"He's lonely and lives by himself. Can I spend some nights with him when I don't have school the next day? Please?" Tony looked with wide eyes at his parents and then back at Samuel.

Samuel nodded yes, that soon Tony could spend the night.

By now, the guests were going into the church hall. They walked into the aromas of pierogis, sausages, sauerkraut, pork, and sweetbreads. The women in town had been cooking for weeks. The music was captivating, and people were beginning to dance to the mazurka. *From the Irish quadrille to the Polish polka . . . I've come a long way.*

Suddenly Tony was by his side. His eyes were on the dancers. "Samuel, there she is. That one."

At that instant, one of the young women grabbed Samuel's arm and pulled him into the circle. He'd been practicing a few steps at home, so he was relaxed and ready to enjoy himself. Tony watched, clapping, and then joined a group of the young children beginning a dance of their own. Everyone in the hall was on their feet dancing until the musicians took a break. The time had come to toast the bride and groom.

Just as the toast was beginning, Samuel took a seat with John, his wife, and another couple. John leaned over and whispered, "You're having a good time."

Samuel, feeling more sophisticated than was his nature, said, "Are you surprised?" as he kicked John under the table. The two shared a secret look, interrupted by Tony.

"Samuel, I saw you dancing with a girl," the boy announced. "Now you're not lonely."

Tony was too big to sit on Samuel's lap anymore, so Samuel bent over and softly said, "Yes, my little friend, not as lonely."

14

After the Benko wedding, many women were excited about Samuel's lace goods. They wanted collars and pendants for Christmas. Samuel wired Emma and Bernadette for another order. He began to think that it might take him less time than he had thought to build up his savings again. He started preparing for the Christmas orders and was soon overjoyed to fill all the requests. The days were full of work, reading, and developing plans for when and where to buy his automobile.

One day after leaving work, he had some free time to write Amina. He wanted to ask his sister how Zawhea was doing. As he composed the lines in his head, he chewed on the tip of the pencil, which led him to make a mental note to order more Blackwing pencils and Parker pens for the store inventory. After finishing the letter and sealing the envelope, he leaned back and began to dream about the future.

A knock at the front door startled him back to reality. Sadie was on the porch, bouncing baby Rima on her hip. "I've brought you Syrian bread."

"Come in. Sit." Samuel cleared a space on the cluttered table. "I could smell the bread as soon as I opened the door. Would you like tea?"

"A small cup. It's cold today, and Rima and I are to meet Anthony and Tony at the market soon. Have I told you how well Tony is doing in school? You must come over tomorrow for Sunday dinner and hear him read."

Samuel put the two cups of tea on the table and lifted Rima in his arms. "I'd love to come to dinner," he said. "I'll bring *malfouf*. Can you believe I actually have ingredients for many of our Syrian dishes but have yet to try to make bread? I've been cooking on Sundays so I'll have food during the week. I have to say, I'm getting good around the kitchen."

"Oh, Samuel, it's good to hear that you're happy living on your own. Your home is welcoming. Are you doing as well as you seem?"

"I think so. I've been enjoying myself. Going to church hall dances. Spending time with John and our friends. Writing letters to my family. In fact, I finished a letter to Amina just before you knocked. Of course, I asked about Zawhea."

"I understand why you miss Zawhea still. On the other hand, it's good that you're getting together with the young people here." Sadie set down her empty cup. "Now I have to go. But we'll see you tomorrow."

Sunday, right after church, Samuel started cooking. He sang as he prepared the cabbage leaves for the *malfouf*. It was one of his favorite dishes. When it was cooked, he left for the Abrahams' home.

Tony opened the door and shouted, "*Umm*, Samuel's here." To Samuel he said, "Can we read the book you brought me? Did you know Beatrix Potter wrote the story? She isn't a potter but an author."

Samuel smiled at Tony's comment. "There isn't a thing I'd like better. But let's wait until after dinner."

"Let me read to you now. Rima's taking a nap. It's hard to read the words when she cries."

So they sat down on the sofa, side by side, and Tony began to read. He stopped whenever he couldn't pronounce a word, and Samuel helped him.

"'Old Mrs. Rabbit was a widow.'" Tony looked up. "What's a widow?" "A widow is a woman who had a husband at one time, but he died." "That's sad. I would cry." Tony kept on. "'She earned her living by knitting rabbit-wool mittens and muffatees.' What are muffatees?"

"I haven't heard that word before. It could be a piece of clothing that goes with mittens. We'll have to ask your *umm*."

Tony kept on until he got tired. Samuel told him, "I helped you with some of the words, but not so many. You've improved. Keep reading books. They're an important part of your education. How old are you?"

"Six. Almost seven." He stood up. "Look how tall I am."

Before Samuel left, he and Anthony set up the times for the spring inventory. They'd bounced back after the robbery, and business was booming. The news of their goods spread to Uniontown, and even though there were competitors in the town, some of the people came to New Salem to buy from them. They were both known as fair, just, and honest. Since some of Uniontown's residents were wealthy, Anthony and Samuel began to carry items such as Tara pocket watches, Waterman ink and ballpoint pens, inkwells, and Lundborg's perfumes. Of course, fabric and the Irish lace goods were also in demand.

THE SYRIAN PEDDLER

Within a month, Anthony would open his store on Main Street, next to the grocer. The plan was to also carry iceboxes, which had just become available. Anthony and Samuel expected to sell a good many of this new convenience, since their customers knew that blocks of ice could be delivered from the icehouse in Uniontown.

Sam's Malfouf

Filling:
1 lb. ground beef or lamb
1 cup rice
Small amount of tomato sauce
1/2 stick butter, melted
1 teaspoon Salt
1/2 teaspoon Pepper
dash of Cinnamon
1/2 teaspoon Allspice 1 medium-sized head of cabbage
Tomato sauce (remainder of 15 oz can)
Lemon

Mix filling ingredients together well. Blanch cabbage by cutting out the stem and putting the whole head in salted, boiling water. As the leaves soften, remove them to a colander to cool. Tear each leaf in half along the middle vein and cut out the heavy center stem. Place about 1 teaspoon o filling along each leaf and roll tightly into the shape of a cigar. Use a trivet in the bottom of your pot to prevent scorching.

Lay the cabbage rolls close together in the pan, changing the direction with each layer. Place an inverted dish on top of the rolls and a cup filled with water on top of the dish to weigh down the rolls. Pour in the rest of the tomato sauce and add water to the top of the rolls. Cover and cook over medium heat for 50-60 minutes. Let sit a few minutes before removing from the pot. Squeeze lemon juice on top, to taste.

15

Samuel awoke early on this Saturday morning in late March. He opened a window, taking in the scent of spring. The leaves were turning green and flowers were starting to bud. It was a new season with the hope of change.

He poured a cup of coffee and sat down to study his notes. In a couple of hours, he would be in Uniontown for the joyful event. *Yes, the white shirt and blue tie will be perfect.*

After dressing slowly and carefully, checking his image, smoothing his hair, he was satisfied. He stepped out the front door, pulled his shoulders back, took a deep breath, and, on the way to the trolley stop, began to sing: 'Sweet land of liberty, of thee I sing . . ."

John was waiting for him. "Good morning. Are you ready for our big day?"

"Believe me, yes. You seem so relaxed, yet look at me." He was jiggling his hands in his pockets, trying to bring on a smile.

When the trolley pulled away, only two seats were empty. Most of the passengers were silent, on their way to work, eyes focused on their newspaper. The remainder talked nervously in pairs.

Soon the trolley entered Uniontown, the county seat. John, Samuel, and many of the other passengers got off at the corner of Second Avenue and Main Street, in front of an imposing, two-story white concrete building. It was the Fayette County Courthouse. Samuel had been there once before, and he was still in awe of its tall columns and cupola-capped tower.

As the men walked up the steps, Samuel noticed the different shades of skin among them. Yes, he and John had the darkest of all. Was he finally used to that? Yes. Did it bother him? A little.

They were ushered into a large room with the American flag, Pennsylvania State flag, and the Fayette County flag on display. A pin hitting the floor could easily have been heard. Looking around the room, Samuel was surprised at the number of men he recognized. He found it strange that not one of them, not even Mr. Benko, had mentioned a word about today.

THE SYRIAN PEDDLER

The judge entered the courtroom. Everyone stood up.

Samuel, John, and everyone else in the room answered the questions with pride, their voices strong. Taking the Oath of Allegiance to the United States of America brought tears to Samuel's eyes and hope for his dreams: a wife, children, and success in his work. Many decades later, he would proudly look back on this moment.

The judge stamped each new citizen's naturalization form and gave him a miniature American flag, along with words of congratulations. He closed the solemn ceremony by welcoming their votes in the next election. Everyone in the room clapped, shook hands, waved their forms and flags in the air.

Samuel and John took the steps two at a time out of the courthouse, laughing. "We're citizens!" John exclaimed. "All our studying these past few months was worth it. I can't believe it. I thought there would be more questions about the United States Constitution."

Samuel smiled. "That surprised me too. And you spent so much time helping me with the facts. American history. The presidents. The laws. We did it together, friend."

The mood of the men when they boarded the trolley was very different. No one was quiet on the way back to New Salem. Samuel closed his eyes and took in the men's remarks, delivered in English with strong Polish, Arabic, Romanian, and Slovakian accents. "Now we really are American." "Who will you vote for next year?" "Our wives and children will be citizens now." "This is a dream come true." "Do you think now we'll be more accepted, even if our skin is a different color?"

None were prepared for what awaited them back home. Some of the men's wives had known when the courthouse was open for swearing-in ceremonies and had spread the word. So when the trolley pulled into the New Salem stop, the new American citizens saw many of the townspeople lined up at the post office, cheering and waving flags, ready to celebrate with them. Their skin color, their religion, their country of origin—none of that mattered. They were one big family now.

John stepped off the trolley and spotted Elena and Margaret in the crowd. He stood tall and waved his flag as he fell into his wife's arms. "My darling," he said, "this was to be my secret surprise for you." Then he picked up Margaret and swung her into the air.

Elena smiled, at the same time shaking her head and folding her arms across her chest. "I wondered what you and Samuel were doing with your noses in books when I would tuck Margaret into bed. Then one day I overheard the postmaster mention the date of the next swearing-in ceremony, and it crossed my mind that maybe—"

"Here we are!" screamed Tony from the crowd.

Samuel received hugs and congratulations from the Abrahams, followed by many others.

"There's cake and ice cream waiting for us in the square," Tony said impatiently. "Let's go."

"And after that," said Sadie, "there's a celebration waiting for you at our house."

Early the next morning, Samuel burst into John's shop waving the *Morning Herald.* "Look. A front-page story about the ceremony. All our names are here." He pointed to the page.

John glanced at it. "I have to take a break and run over to the market to pick up a copy. Before they're all gone."

"No need. I have two papers. One for you."

"Thank you, Samuel. Remember to send the clipping home so your *abb* and *umm* can read about your citizenship."

"Yes. But not right away. There's still a lot to do, and we're only days away from opening the store."

16

A wealthy developer from Uniontown had finished two small buildings on Center Street to entice new businesses to open in New Salem.

Anthony had purchased one of them, two shops down from the post office. He and Samuel thought it was a perfect location. Also, it had a brick front with one display window and a small room in the back for an office.

Today they were stocking the fabric and shoe shelves. They'd finished putting the lace, the watches, pens, pencils, and perfumes in the enclosed glass cases under the countertop. Bolts of fabric would go on the lowest shelves so customers could feel the different choices from linens to cottons. Shoes and boots would be displayed on the next shelves, with the boxes stored beneath each style. On the other side of the store were work clothes and undergarments. Just to the left of the front door were two iceboxes. Customers had been waiting impatiently for these to be available, and Abraham's would keep two in stock and take orders for more.

"Sadie is coming to help us after she gets Tony at school," Anthony told Samuel. "She plans to do the window displays. If you and I work through lunch, we could be finished with the shelves before Tony gets here. Otherwise, he'll want to help us and we'll never get done."

"Understood. I'm off to buy cheese and meat to eat with the bread you brought. It won't take me long. And we can eat while we work."

Later, as they were admiring the stocked shelves, Tony burst in the door followed by Sadie carrying Rima. "Look at the store!" he shouted. "It's ours!"

Anthony bent down and gave him a hug. "Son, you can help your *umm* with the window display if you listen to her instructions."

They'd decided to keep the display simple: an American flag, work boots, shoes, lace, fabric, and patterns that they hoped would attract both men and women. As they began, Tony climbed in the window and arranged pairs of men's work boots, black patent Mary Janes, and women's pumps. Sadie draped light blue and floral cotton fabric over stacked shoeboxes then leaned several Butterick dress patterns against the fabric with matching thread and a lace collar. Then she added a smart-looking wide-brimmed hat decorated with lace ribbon.

Anthony watched them work as he hung the sign: "Abraham's Dry Goods." After he and Sadie admired the window and sign from the sidewalk, they walked into the back room to check on Rima. Samuel was sweeping up the floor of the main area. All three heard Tony shriek loudly, "Samuel, look at me. This is fun." He was almost to the top of the rolling ladder used to stock the shelves. And he was about to roll.

Samuel rushed over to him and said quietly, "You aren't tall enough or old enough to be on this ladder. I'm going to hold it still so you can climb back down. And I'm here to catch you if you fall."

Tony made it to the bottom. "I won't do that again until I'm ten years old."

"Good boy. How about sleeping at my house tonight?"

"I'm sleeping at Samuel's tonight!" Tony's shrill voice could be heard from the sidewalk. Out front, the horses perked up their ears in excitement.

Anthony had seen everything from the door. He marched to his son and said, "If you want to help me in the store, you have to behave. Samuel is right. You could hurt yourself on the ladder. Now quiet down if you want to spend the night with Samuel."

Tony hung his head. "I'm sorry," he mumbled.

Sadie walked in from the back of the store with Rima in her arms. She and Anthony both looked at Tony, trying hard to appear stern. Then they glanced at each other, doing their best not to laugh at their son's excitement.

Abraham's Dry Goods opened the next day. Sadie was serving Arabic *ahweh* and *baklava* to the customers. Tony was trying to help, and Rima was napping in the back room. Samuel stood watching and thinking about all the work they'd accomplished. *I'll have my own store sometime in the next few years, but first—my Ford.* He and Anthony had a gentlemen's agreement regarding the profits. Samuel would still peddle to customers on Mondays, Tuesdays, and Wednesdays. The rest of the week, he would work in the store.

After the opening, the store stayed bustling. Farm families came to buy shoes, fabric, and work clothes. Many of the coal miners preferred Anthony's store to their company store. Within six months they were very successful, and Samuel was amazed at his savings.

THE SYRIAN PEDDLER

17

May 8, 1907
Dear Samuel,

We are so proud of you. All the success you are having with the business—selling the Irish lace, opening the new store with Anthony. All good news.

I am afraid that I have no good news in return. The fighting continues between the Ottomans and our home country. The Ottomans are continuing to raise taxes for us Christians to try to force us out. Abb and I think about moving to France, but we know we are still not ready to leave our beloved Syria.

There is more unhappy news. Zawhea's husband died in March during one of the attempts to overthrow the opposition. Her baby boy, Mitelj, is almost a year old, and she is with a second child, soon to be born. She lives with her parents now.

Son, I know you had feelings for Zawhea, and you may still. You could write to Amina if you want to send Zawhea your condolences.

We miss you greatly,
Umm

Sam read the letter repeatedly until he had memorized the words. *Zawhea with no husband and two babies. What will she do? I have to write her.*

After much deep thought and prayer, he sat down at the kitchen table to write two letters, the second one a great deal more difficult to compose than the first.

June 4, 1907
My dear Amina,

Umm wrote about Zawhea's husband. I have enclosed a letter to her. Please see that she receives this, as well as my address.

THE SYRIAN PEDDLER

*You knew I was sad about her arranged marriage, and now I would
like to be in touch with her.*
Salaam,
Samuel

Dear Zawhea,
    *Umm wrote to me about the death of your husband. Please
accept my condolences, and know that I am sad for you. She told me
about your little boy, Mitelj, and that soon you will have a second
child.*
    *Ever since the Abrahams had a baby girl—an event that
made little Tony very happy—I have rented a small home of my
own. You would like it. There is a parlor and small kitchen. My
bedroom is comfortable. There is running water and a small bath
area. I try to make my home like my umm's as much as possible,
and I am even cooking with Syrian spices. (You would like my
malfouf, I think.) I found some bright pillows with gold and blue at
the market to adorn my couch. People from my church helped me
when I moved. They gave me dishes and cooking pots, and now they
busy themselves trying to find me a wife. Yet none of the women here
interest me.*
    *Zawhea, you know that I understood and respected your
marriage. However, there isn't a woman I have met who would
please me more than you would. I know it is too soon for you to
decide. Yet, as time goes on, and after your baby is born, will you
think about coming to America to be my wife? No doubt, you will
ask yourself whether I can support you and your children. Anthony
has recently opened his own store. I work there and peddle goods in
the nearby towns and countryside. The coal mining industry has been
good for business, and our customers are buying more goods—
including ink pens, expensive watches, and fancy clothing—than
ever before. My goal is to open my own store.*
*I miss you and pray that you will come to America. I await your
answer.*
Salaam,
Saddo

He read the letter several times. *Yes, it's good that I told Zawhea I care for her and want her to come be with me.* After receiving his *umm's* letter, he'd had time to think it through and be sure of the words he would write.

He sealed the envelope and walked to the post office. *It's done. Now I wait for her response.*

The summer passed slowly as he waited for Zawhea to reply. He started writing in his journal again. His first entry was a list of things to do.

1. Pray more—daily
2. Pittsburgh trip for inventory—August
3. Save, save, save
4. Curtains for the kitchen—see if Elena will sew them for me
5. New bedcover and towels
6. Bookcase—build it
7. My own store in Masontown—work on a business plan
8. Pray more
9. Ford Model F
10. Keep my proposal to Zawhea a secret—for now

On a sultry day in August, Samuel started off on his buying trip. It was on the return trip this time that he would stop over in Pittsburgh to make most of the purchases. But his first stop was New York City to buy more lace goods. Of course, he could have ordered those by post. But the truth was that he hoped to see Emma.

The train arrived just in time to make it to the hotel for dinner. Samuel hopped on the trolley and soon was in front of the hotel. By now, he could afford a room there. It was approaching late afternoon when he walked up to the front desk. Yes, he was told, the shop was about to close, but he had a few minutes

Only Emma's cousin was inside, straightening merchandise on the shelves. "Good afternoon, Bernadette," Samuel greeted her. "How are you?"

"Hello, Samuel. I'm doing well, thank you. It's been a long time. Emma told me your business finally recovered from that horrible robbery."

"Yes, business is good. . . . I've come to buy additional pieces. And I want to make sure our agreement is still in place."

"Certainly. We honor all our agreements. Emma and I appreciate your business." She looked at the shop entrance then at Samuel. "Let me show you our newest pieces." She put a hand on his arm to lead him to a display.

"These new lace bands are very well done," Samuel said. "Let's add a dozen of them to the order I have ready here. They'll go nicely with the hats we sell. Can I pick up the merchandise in the morning before I leave for Pittsburgh?" "Of course. I'll have your order ready by mid-morning. We want nothing more than to please."

"I'll have the money order when I come." He stifled a yawn. "Now I'm going to my room to rest. Train travel can be tiring, you know. Please tell your parents and Emma I send my best wishes."

"Emma should be here soon. She's playing this evening." "Well, now. . . . until tomorrow, Bernadette." *Perfect.* He left the shop and went up to his room.

On the way to the dining room, Samuel passed the café where Emma was playing. She hadn't yet glanced his way, so he sat down and ordered a glass of *arak*. At the end of the next song, she rose from the piano bench to take a break in the hall.

He followed her. When he was close enough, he called, "Emma, wait." She stopped and slowly turned around, then stared at him in disbelief.

"What are you doing here? And why didn't you send a telegram letting me know when you'd arrive?"

"I had to see you one last time. And I was fearful you wouldn't agree to it *Rajaa'an*, don't be angry with me."

After glancing around and not seeing anyone, he moved closer to her and said, "I wanted to tell you I understand—and that I'm not angry with you. . . . Oh, at first I was. But I've come to realize that our cultures really are miles apart."

She slowly pulled away. "You're a wonderful, hard-working, handsome, and considerate man. It's just that—oh, I don't know how to explain. And now I have to get back to playing."

"Don't explain. You said it all in your letter."

He went back to his table and glass of *arak*. Emma stood still, watching him for a moment, before she sat at the piano. He listened to a few pieces then went to the dining room.

In the morning, Samuel walked into the shop feeling good about last evening and his conversation with Emma. Once again, only Bernadette was there. "Good morning," he told her.

She leaned over the counter, gazing at him, her eyelashes fluttering. "It is a good morning. Perfect weather. And you look particularly handsome." She strolled around the counter, lifting a corner of her skirt at the same time. "Can I get you a cup of coffee?"

"I'd welcome that. I haven't had breakfast."

Bernadette returned with coffee and a scone. They both leaned against the counter as he sipped the inferior liquid. She moved, little by little, closer to him until her right arm touched his left arm. Then she turned to him and put her hand on his shoulder. He moved away. She moved closer. He moved again.

She said, her voice low, "You know Emma has another man in her life. And you? Do you have another woman?"

"Uh, I prefer not to say. I *will* tell you that I'm preparing to buy an automobile."

"An automobile! Then you can drive back here soon to visit me."

Just then, Emma walked in. With her hands on her hips, she directed an icy stare toward her cousin.

Bernadette grimaced, straightened her back. "I'll put the order in a parcel for you, Samuel. Then you can be on your way."

Emma smiled. "Did I hear the word 'automobile'?"

"You did," Samuel replied. "I'm planning to buy a Ford Model F. There was one parked outside the hotel a while back. A fine-looking one, I have to say." He turned to leave. "I wish I had more time, but I'm running late. Now I have to hurry to catch my train. You ladies take care of yourselves."

On his way home, he thought of Emma and Zawhea. Then he opened the latest issue of *The World's Work*.

18

Samuel had been in America for two years and three months when he climbed into his Model F and started the motor. He laughed until he thought his head would fall off. John was laughing with him, since he'd just ordered the same car.

"John, we did it," Samuel said. "We're citizens. And now we bought our own autos."

"We're a good team," John said and slapped Samuel on the back.

It was five o'clock, a perfect time to stop by the tavern. They shared a drink with several other men in town who were already automobile owners, ready to toast John's and Samuel's good fortune.

Samuel leaned back in his chair. He couldn't stop smiling as he silently counted the many more calls he could make in a day on his route. The vehicle would pay for itself soon enough. On the spot, he decided to name her "Maggie."

Sam enjoyed Sundays after church, when he could polish Maggie and take a drive in the country. Often on these leisurely excursions, he found himself thinking of Zawhea. Yes, he still hoped for a letter that would answer his prayers. *An automobile can't take the place of a good woman.*

One October day, after many calls, many deliveries, Samuel stopped at the post office. Lately he'd been checking the mail often. This day the letter from Zawhea had arrived.

He tried to remain calm until he got home. Once inside, he opened the envelope, his hands trembling. He sat down at the table and read and read and read the letter.

October 5, 1907
Dear Saddo,
  I hope this letter finds you well.

I have been healing since my husband's death. My parents moved to Aleppo to help me with the babies. Amina comes to visit often. I was happy when she brought me your letter, and I told her about your proposal. For days, I read your letter many times. As you may know, I was not happy about my arranged marriage. Abraham was good to me, but you were always first in my heart.

I am touched by your proposal. Yes, I will be your wife. And my joy is made greater by having my parents' blessing.

Amina and Zacharias will travel with me to America. She will write to you about our plans. I pray every day for a safe journey into your arms.

My baby arrived healthy. Her name is Martha. Umm and Abb want me to leave my children with them, as many babies die during the ocean crossing. I love my babies dearly, but I do think that leaving them here until we can bring them safely to America is best.

Please send me your thoughts. I want to please your wishes. I await your letter.

Salaam,
Zawhea

He bowed his head. *Inshallah.* He kissed the envelope and put the letter in his pocket. *What will I do now? What first? Oh, my journal list? Right. Whom shall I tell? John, yes? No, not now. He'll be home with his family. But Anthony will still be at the store, closing it for the night*

He sprinted down Main Street and arrived just in time. Anthony was alone. Samuel let out a shout. "She said yes."

"Yes for what? Who is 'she'?"

"I asked Zawhea to marry me. I just received her letter."

"What wonderful news! Come home with me for dinner. You can share your joy with Sadie and Tony. *Msayyar mish mkhayya.* Life is ordained."

And so it began, reviewing his list, finishing the bookshelf, crossing items off one by one, and smiling a hundred smiles as he crossed off the tenth item.

Everyone who knew Samuel understood his methodical approach to all he did. It wasn't surprising how he proceeded with the plans for Zawhea's arrival. The community heard about his bride-to-be. Tony told all his school friends. Samuel had done his part to share the news with his friends. John and Elena were ecstatic. Mrs. Benko couldn't stop crying happy tears for him. Sadie— well, Sadie seemed the happiest of all.

A letter from Amina arrived shortly after the one from Zawhea.

October 6, 1907
Dear Samuel,

We will be sailing with Zawhea on November 15. Umm and Abb are so happy for you. We all love Zawhea.

Zacharias is thinking we may settle in Pittsburgh and not return to Syria. It is good to immigrate now—before we have our babies. One day we may all go visit our country again. We have been trying to convince Abb and Umm to go with us. Yet they say they are so rooted in Syria that it would be very difficult to give it up and start a new life in America.

They are so proud of you, my brother. Let us pray, once we have families, that they will sail over for a visit.

If all goes well on our voyage, we will arrive around December 4. As you suggested, we have arranged for quarters in first class. Rajaa'an, reserve lodging for us in New Salem. We will be there to help you plan the wonderful event—the wedding. Zawhea is very, very happy.
Salaam,
Amina

October 15, 1907
Dear Zawhea,

You will soon be in my arms as my bride. I have given much thought to bringing the children over with you. Your abb and umm are right. They are able and willing to provide a safe and stable home, to give them a strong foundation and opportunities for schooling Your children should stay living there until they are older and can make the trip safely. I understand that it will be hard for you to leave them.

Amina's letter arrived the day after yours. I am so glad that she and Zacharias will travel with you.

After you disembark on Ellis Island, you will go through the registration. I will be waiting for you there. We will then take the train to Pittsburgh and change to go on to Uniontown. Then we have a short drive to New Salem, where Anthony will meet us. Bring only a small bag. We can buy what you need here.

Stay strong. It is good that you will be leaving on November 15. I do not want you crossing in winter weather.

I will wire you money tomorrow.
Sending my love,
Saddo

Samuel mailed the letter then sent telegrams to Zawhea and Amina. This way, even if the letter were delayed, they'd get word that he would be meeting them on Ellis Island—and be assured that he'd arranged for their stay in New Salem. Most of all, he wanted Zawhea to know he agreed about leaving Mitelj and Martha with her parents and that he was eagerly awaiting her arrival.

One Sunday in November, Samuel walked to the Nazzifs' house for dinner. He was bursting with news. In his pocket was a telegram from Zawhea that he wanted to share with John. "I bring you my famous *malfouf*," he said, as soon as he was inside. "And can you imagine what else?"

John laughed. "I never know with you. If I were to guess, you heard from Zawhea."

"Yes She plans to leave Marseilles with Amina and Zacharias on November 15. They should arrive on December 4." Samuel was shaking his head in disbelief that she would soon be with him.

John hugged him and slapped him on the back. "Your dream has come true. I'm happy for you, my friend."

Elena had overheard their conversation from the kitchen. She gave Samuel a hug. "Now we can plan for the wedding. . . . Wait here." She left the room and came back holding a set of curtains. "I finally finished them. The fabric was a dream to sew with. And I had extra blue trim from another project. What do you think?"

"They'll be perfect for the kitchen. With these, I'm almost ready for Zawhea's arrival. The bookshelves lack only staining. It'll be good to get my stacks of books off the floor."

"You've become an avid fan of American history," John said. "What are you reading now?"

"*The Naval War of 1812* by Theodore Roosevelt. I'll lend it to you when I'm done. Yet of all the books I've read so far, my favorite is *The Rough Riders*, also by President Roosevelt."

For the next two months Samuel was busy making sure he and Anthony had holiday inventory. He'd just ordered more pocket watches from Saehan. The customers liked to place their gift orders before Thanksgiving. Many had to budget and would pay upon delivery right before Christmas. Now, Samuel began to plan his finances that would accommodate a wife and children. *This is my third Christmas in America, and my bride will be here with me on Christmas Day. Inshallah.*

By Thanksgiving, Samuel had become very anxious. He was having dinner with the Abrahams, but his mind was elsewhere.

"Samuel, did you hear me?" Sadie asked. "Would you like coffee?"

"Sorry. My head is in the clouds. All I can think of is being ready to greet my bride. The date is fast approaching. Yes. Coffee, please."

"But your home is lovely, and Zawhea will be happy there. So don't worry."

"I can't help it. I guess it's my nature."

"Come visit us anytime and we can talk—before and after Zawhea arrives. Anthony and I will help you in any way."

"I know, Sadie. You and Anthony are family."

Tony bounded into the room. "Samuel, what's going to happen after you're married? Can I still visit?"

"Of course you can. You're like my little brother, remember?" "Samuel, can I call you Sam? 'Samuel' is a long name." "Why, I like that. Yes, call me Sam."

From that day on, Samuel was known as 'Sam' in and around New Salem.

PART II

Samuel and Anna

"If there be any truer measure of a man than by what he does, it must be by what he gives."

ROBERT SOUTH

19

The first Sunday in December Sam was about to leave the church when he remembered the appointment with Father Salim. He planned to skip the church social—so much to do. Back in the church hall, he stopped to get a cup of coffee when . . . "Are you ready for your bride? Is it true your sister and her husband are coming too?"

"Mrs. Jawdy, I'm almost ready. And I'm in a bit of a rush today." He turned abruptly toward the church office. *Thought I could get by without any questions. That's impossible. Whatever she hears will be the talk around town tomorrow.*

Though Sam had had many conversations with Father Salim, his stomach was doing somersaults as he knocked on the door.

"Come in. Good to see you," Father said. He motioned to a chair and turned to his desk to gather papers.

After he sat down, Sam took comfort in the painting above the desk. It was of St. Ellien, one of his favorites. He'd always been comfortable in Father's office, but today was different—yes, different.

Sipping his coffee, Father began. "Tell me about your bride-to-be."

"I've known Zawhea since I was in grammar school," Sam replied. "Our families celebrated the Syrian holidays together. I always had feelings for her. She still had a year of school to complete when I left to come to America."

"As often as we've talked, I don't recall hearing what brought you to America. Did your parents encourage your emigration?"

"They wanted the best for me. So they arranged for Anthony to meet me when I arrived. You see, Anthony had apprenticed with my father in the export business. I've dreamed of being here ever since Anthony left Damascus."

"Anthony has done well, as have you. Your store is always busy. By the way, my wife loves the lace you sell."

"All the women do. I met the designer during the crossing. She and her cousin sell their lace designs at a hotel shop in Manhattan. . . . But back to my love. We've been writing to each other. After she finished school, she wrote to say that her parents had arranged for her to marry. I didn't have the savings to bring Zawhea over and start a family. I was, as you might say, heartbroken."

"Not an unusual story. Most Syrian men come here to begin a productive life and save to bring loved ones over. We don't want our young women making the voyage only to face hardship and disappointment when they arrive."

"I understand that. . . . But it's still hard to accept—her marriage." He rubbed his hands on his knees.

"Mind if I smoke my pipe?" Father began to tamp the tobacco into the bowl.

"No . . . reminds me of my father. He smokes a briar pipe packed with Latakia tobacco."

"Latakia is too strong for me. I mix it with an English blend."

"One of these days, I'll buy a pipe. I wonder if we should carry them in the store."

"Good idea. That would save me a trip to The Tobacconist in Uniontown." Sam took another sip of his coffee. "One day, my mother wrote to tell me that Zawhea's husband had died in one of the revolts and left her with two babies."

"Let me guess. You wrote to her?"

"I still loved her. After a time, I did write to ask her to be my bride. We've agreed that the children should stay with her parents for now. It would be too dangerous for the little ones on that ship." He stood and began to pace, his hands in his pockets. "There's one more thing. I wonder if I'll be, how should I say, as good as her first husband."

"I wouldn't worry. If you hadn't emigrated you might have married her at home. Think of this as a new beginning for you both."

"Yes, it will be. But I'm also worried about her leaving her babies behind. She may have a hard time here without them."

"You could discuss that with Zawhea and come up with a plan to bring them over. That may help her." Father glanced down at his calendar, rubbing his chin. "The Saturdays in December are open. After she arrives, come see me and we'll finalize the date."

"Thank you, Father." Before leaving, he noticed Father's smile. *Everything will be good if I can just relax.*

While Sam worked in the store the next day, he felt like it would never end. Tomorrow, he would leave to meet the S.S. *Neustria.*

When he finally got home, he swept the front steps and porch—all the time remembering his voyage on the same ship. Once finished, he went inside and walked through each room, wondering what Zawhea would think of his home.

A repeated knock and someone calling "Sam, are you here?" interrupted his thoughts. It was Elena. She'd come in the unlocked front door. "I wasn't sure you were home since you didn't answer."

He made a large sweeping motion with his arm. "How does it look?" "Lovely." She went over to the bookcase and moved a few books around. Then she stood back with her hands on her hips. "Now it looks even better. I've brought you dinner."

"You know me. I might forget to eat . . . can't keep my mind still . . . thinking about her arrival. Where can I buy flowers for the table?"

"I'm not sure about flowers. Since the freeze, mine are gone. I'll cut some pine with berries and bring them over. Do you have a vase?"

"A vase? Why would I have a vase?"

Elena laughed. "Never you mind. Remember to give John your spare key. I'll bring some pine in a vase before you get back. Now I've got to leave."

"Thank you for everything. I'd have forgotten to make that appointment with Father Salim if you hadn't reminded me."

"Yes, lately you *have* been hopeless at times. Try to eat some food, and then rest up for tomorrow."

After dinner, Sam packed a small bag with a change of clothes. In his socks he put the beloved replica of his church and some extra cash. In no time at all he'd be on the train to meet his family.

The morning sky was still dark when Sam woke. He dressed in a warm sweater with work trousers, then sat in the kitchen and went over what was to happen the next few days. Soon John pulled up in front of his house. After one last look around, he picked up his bag and made sure he had his money holder and the key for John.

It was a cold morning, and the station, being tiny, had only outside seating. Sam said, getting out of John's automobile, "Twenty minutes before my train arrives."

"I've time to wait with you," his friend said. "Let's get coffee and a paper." They sat on the benches, sipping the hot liquid, feeling the warmth of their cups. John broke the silence. "Why so quiet?"

"I'm thinking I should turn around and go home. What if this doesn't work?"

"Don't let me down, my friend. It'll work. How long have you been waiting for this day? Try to think about the time—"

Sam never heard the rest, since the train's whistle overpowered John's voice. He stood and shook John's hand. "See you in a few days."

The train was crowded, passengers going to the big city to shop or maybe to meet loved ones. Sam sat down and unfolded the paper. The headline caught his attention—**President Roosevelt Prepares to Enact Hague Convention Treaties**. He admired Theodore Roosevelt and read all he could about him. Later, his thoughts drifted to his school in Damascus, the brownstone front with the many steps where he would sit with his friends, practicing English and talking about America. Before long, he'd dozed off.

He awoke as the train approached Penn Station. The Nadars were expecting him to spend the night.

Heavy snow was falling in the late evening when Sam knocked lightly on the Nadars' door. George was waiting with two glasses of *arak*. "Samuel, *Marhaba*. Come in. Come in. Rose left some bread, za'atar, cheese, and *kibbeh*. You're hungry, eh?"

"It's been a long, cold day," he said, shivering and taking off his coat.

"You'll be warm soon. I've heard good news about your business from Anthony—and, of course, now the wedding. We have much to celebrate. To your good fortune."

They raised their glasses.

"Ah, George, God is with me."

Sam woke early and bathed, humming as he dressed in a white shirt and blue tie. *This is the big day.* After packing, he went downstairs with his bag and coat in hand.

"George, are you off to work?" he asked his host, who was walking toward the front door.

"I've a busy day ahead—but not as exciting as yours. Rose has breakfast for you. It's been good to see you, despite how brief the visit was. You take care of yourself and your bride-to-be."

Sam walked to the kitchen. "Good morning," he greeted Rose. "Did I wake you last night? I arrived late."

"No. I didn't even hear the two of you talking. Do you have time to tell me about your wedding plans?"

"The ship will be in port at noon, so I should leave in the next hour. But, yes, there's time. The wedding plans? Zawhea and I will decide everything together. But I hope it's before Christmas."

"This is good news. And how is Sadie?"

"She's well. Busy with the family. And with the store, since she does most of our accounting. Rima has started walking, and Tony's now in third grade."

"They grow so fast. My youngest will finish her schooling this year. Then I'll be able to help George more in the store. Did he tell you we bought a few pieces of Emma's lace for Christmas gifts?" "No, I don't think we got around to that."

"Emma told us she's planning to wed an Irish railroad engineer from Altoona, Pennsylvania. I wonder how that dear girl will like living in a small town."

Sam rubbed his chin. "She talked often about having the lace shop and living in her own apartment. I'm surprised she's marrying. Yet now it's been almost three years since she arrived on Ellis Island." *Three years since I've seen Zawhea. I wonder if she still looks the same, with her long, dark, silky hair and those eyes . . . she could only grow more beautiful.*

On the trolley to the ferry landing, he overheard a couple speaking Arabic. He thought about his first language, which he wanted his children to learn. *These days, the only time I speak Arabic is with my non-English speaking Syrian customers. There's no one to talk to at home . . . yet.*

Within the hour, the ferry had come to a stop at Ellis Island. Sam bolted up the path to the registry door. People were bustling around, looking for family, bags, or the telegraph post. He stopped, panting, at the bottom of the staircase leading upstairs where the immigrants were to go to checkpoints. Then he pulled out a comb, straightened his tie, and took a deep breath. At the top of the stairs he spotted Amina and Zacharias in line. His heart beat like a drum, faster, faster, as he raced to Amina, hugged her, and frantically asked, "Where is she?"

"My dear brother. In one of the exam rooms having her eyes checked. We said we'd meet at baggage."

"What if she doesn't pass?" *I never thought of this. I need to find her.* "What room number?"

"Room Ten."

When Sam found the room, there were many people waiting in line for their exam and no place to sit. He wandered around for a while, thinking about the day he experienced the Great Hall for the first time. *I was a boy at seventeen, and now I'm a man, a naturalized citizen who's about to marry.* Once at baggage claim, he resigned himself to waiting, sitting on a bench. There he watched, tapping his feet and looking longingly at every young woman who passed by.

Zawhea walked out of the exam room, puzzled about where to go next. She followed the arrows down the stairs to the checkout stations. *Which way? These arrows confuse me.* She stopped at the telegraph post and asked, "Sir, where is baggage claim?"

"Go to the dining hall and turn to your left."

"*Shukran.*"

She spotted him first from a distance and paused to smooth out her ruffled blouse and deep-blue gored tweed skirt—the best a woman could without a mirror.

Samuel felt a gentle tap on the shoulder and heard her sweet voice. "Saddo."

He turned with misted eyes and saw hers, dark as onyx, along with her shining curly hair and the smile he'd kept in his heart.

"Zawhea. It's really you."

"The medical examiner suspected an infection in my left eye. But it seems to be only redness from the wind at sea."

He hugged her for a full minute and then stood back, holding her hands and looking into her eyes. "You're here now and soon to be my wife. I was beginning to worry. I waited outside the exam room and then decided to come here. Amina told me you were to meet by the baggage area. How was the voyage? Did you get sick?"

"The seas weren't rough. Only one day did I feel ill. I was grateful to be in first class."

Sam, at five feet ten inches, was five inches taller than Zawhea. He moved his hands to her shoulders, pulled her closer for another hug, and bent down to kiss each cheek. "You look beautiful."

If Amina hadn't come to them, they might still be there in the same spot. "You found each other. We couldn't check your bags out. It's simple, since the lines are organized according to the ship and the class we traveled in. Saddo, you'll be happy to know we all packed lightly as you advised."

He hugged his sister and Zacharias. "Sorry for my rush when I first spotted you. I was in such a hurry to find Zawhea. You all must be tired. Let's rest before we board the ferry."

Bags in hand, the four agreed to go into the dining hall for a simple meal of porridge and bread before leaving for Manhattan.

After they were seated, Amina commented, "I'm amazed and pleased at all the services they provide us immigrants in this Great Hall."

"From banking to dining to sending telegrams," said Sam.

"It's surprising to me too," Zawhea said as their food arrived. "Now that I'm on solid ground, I have an appetite." She paused before she took the first bite. "Saddo, I haven't had time to tell you, but I've decided to go by my middle name, Anna, since they listed that first on my entrance papers. You can still call me Zawhea, if you'd like."

"No, I like 'Anna.' It fits you well. Talking about names, quite a while ago I'd changed 'Saddo' to 'Samuel,' and then recently Tony started calling me 'Sam.' Now most of my friends do the same."

"I like that. Sam and Anna," Zawhea, now Anna, said quietly.

"I've made reservations at Bridget Bolling's boarding house for tonight," Sam announced. "In the morning, we'll take the train to Pittsburgh and then on to Uniontown."

Snow was lightly falling. As they boarded the ferry to Manhattan, Sam gazed at the Statue of Liberty. "She looks so different than on the summer day when I arrived—only because of the swirls of snow around her. But she's always regal. Always inspiring."

"She is. Look at her. More magnificent than in any pictures," Anna said. "And the city in the distance—tell us about it."

"The city can't compare to our Damascus, with its majestic buildings and churches rich in history. New York City is a mix of many cultures. The immigrants try to live in communities with people of their own kind."

"Are you saying that the Syrians settle in homes in the same area?"

"Yes. My friends, the Nadars, live in an area called Little Syria where many Syrians live, some sharing apartments."

Amina chimed in. "What can we expect to see on the streets?"

THE SYRIAN PEDDLER

"There are peddlers, speakeasies, hotels, and shops. People get around the city by trolley cars, automobiles, and still by horse and buggy. They all seem to be in a hurry to get somewhere." He watched his family looking at the far-off, unknown city and remembered his feelings when he first set foot on American soil. *I never thought I'd be happier than on that day. Yet today I am. She's the same as I remember. . . . What am I going to do tonight when she's in the room next to me?*

From the ferry landing in Manhattan, they walked the two blocks to the trolley stop. When they got there, Sam heard the dreaded words again: "What do you Negroes think you're doing here?" *I should have warned Anna.*

The four of them stopped as three men came from behind to face them. Sam stepped toward the men and said, "You're mistaken. We're Christians from Syria who've arrived here to make our way to a better life. Leave us alone and we'll not bother you." He stared at them directly and calmly until they turned and walked away, grumbling, in the other direction.

Until that moment, the city had been a remarkable sight with an astounding variety of people and storefronts. Now Anna stood frozen in her steps. "Saddo . . . Samuel, why didn't you do more to protect us? I'm not sure I want to be here in this country. You never said this might happen. No. You didn't warn me at all."

Sam looked forlorn. "Ah, you're right. It's something I should have told you. I'm sorry. This has happened to me a couple of times since I arrived. Those men are bigots. They detest Negroes. And I hear it's even more serious in the South."

"At least they didn't hurt us. Or rob us," Zacharias said, putting his arm around Anna. "Sam was able to deter them."

Amina looked at her brother. "I never thought I'd be mistaken for a Negro."

"I felt the same," Sam told her. "It took me a while to realize that many consider our skin dark and so they react to us as they do to black people. I've worked on being patient and keeping my temper under control. Today I was able to do that. Don't worry. We'll be fine."

"You may be used to this," said Anna, "but I'm not. It'll take time to forget this happened to me on my first day in America."

Sam hugged her. "We *could* walk. We're not far from the boarding home. But let's take the trolley since we have the bags. And I want you to save your energy."

106

The trolley soon turned onto a small side street where there were several boarding houses, conveniently located for travelers.

"Mrs. Bolling, I'm Samuel Hanna checking in for three rooms. This is my sister, Amina, her husband, Zacharias, and my wife-to-be, Anna."

"Welcome to my home, all of you. Enough of the formalities. Call me Bridget. My guests are like family to me." The smiling woman handed out keys. "Your rooms are the first three at the top of the staircase. You go freshen up. Dinner will be at six o'clock."

As Sam carried Anna's bags into her room, they looked longingly at each other. "Where do you want these?" he asked.

"By the chair. I only need to use the smaller one this evening. Sam, do you mind if I rest before dinner? We have so much to talk about, but I'm tired."

He touched her cheek gently. "Yes, you should rest, my darling. We can talk later. Remember, we have the rest of our lives together."

"You better knock on my door at five-thirty, lest I sleep through dinner."

This is too much of a temptation. He went across the hall to his own room. An hour later, he dressed then knocked on Anna's door. "Are you ready for dinner?"

"Not quite, Sam. I'll see you in the dining room."

"Take your time."

After a pot roast dinner, the boarders retreated to the sitting room for coffee, tea, and brandy. There, the conversation centered on travel and the wonders of New York City. The remaining three boarders had traveled to America from Ireland and had been there for a week. Of course, Sam knew quite a bit about their country but didn't say much. After all, what he knew he'd learned from Emma and her relatives—and Emma was far from his mind tonight.

While the others talked, he couldn't keep his eyes off Anna. She wore a ruby-red frock, the bodice trimmed with pearl buttons down to the waistline, with a flouncy skirt that flared just above her ankle. He could see a bit of her black stockings, since she'd changed from high-laced boots to black pumps with pearl buckles. With her slim figure, her hair pulled back in a chignon, her flawless skin, and her eyes that lit up when she smiled, she was gorgeous.

"Sam, did you hear me?"

"Sorry, Amina," he said. "I was thinking about our, uh, train schedule for the morning."

"Ah, yes. We have to rise early. I think I'll turn in."

Everyone agreed as they finished their drinks and said goodnight.

Sam tossed and turned for quite a while.

In the room across the hall, Anna was also tossing and turning. Then, in the middle of her dream, she sat upright. *Where am I? Where are my babies?* Rubbing her eyes, she got out of bed to turn on the light. *I really am in America with Sam. I'm worried about this. I love him but—*

There was a knock on the door.

"It's me. Sam."

Anna thought about what to do. She threw on her robe and tiptoed to the door. "Come in," she whispered. The two stood nervously looking at each other.

"Anna, can we talk?"

"Yes." She motioned toward the only chair in the room.

He sat down, and she perched on the end of the bed—waiting. He nervously rubbed his pant leg, a habit of his during stress. Finally he said, "It took time for me to understand that I loved you as early as Amina's wedding."

"I had a feeling. At first, you were like the brother I never had. But then I realized my feelings were deeper. I cried myself to sleep when my parents arranged my marriage."

"My dear, I couldn't bring you here any sooner. I needed to be sure I could take care of you and our children to come."

"I know and understand. My first husband got so involved in preparing for the Young Turks movement. I wonder if he *ever* loved me or the babies."

"I'm sorry to hear this, Anna." He moved to the edge of the bed. Anna didn't resist as he gently kissed her cheek, taking a deep breath of the sandalwood she so loved to dab on her neck.

"You're wearing one of my favorite scents."

"I am. I also love amber oil. Can I buy them in New Salem?"

"In Uniontown. . . . I never thought of this before, but we should carry the oils in the store."

She yawned. "I'm looking forward to seeing the store and meeting your friends."

"You will soon. Now we both need sleep."

Early Thursday morning they boarded the train at Penn Station. When on their way, Sam said, "Amina, how are our parents?"

"They never change. Always working hard and seemingly healthy. They've missed you—and now they'll miss me."

"In my letters I've tried to convince them to visit."

"You know, they just can't leave their business and their country. Your letters gave them pleasure, though. They're proud of you."

"I worry about them with the unrest."

Zacharias interrupted. "It *is* worrisome, and it's not getting any better." At that moment, Anna leaned her head on Sam's shoulder and whispered,

"I wonder if my parents will bring my babies over to live with us. I miss them." "My dear," Sam whispered back, "try not to worry about them now. We'll talk about a plan when we get home."

"Home. My new home." Just as she said this, they pulled into the Pittsburgh station and changed trains to go to Uniontown.

Once they were settled in their seats, Sam told them about his own trip from Ellis Island to New Salem. He described his stay with Anthony's brother in Pittsburgh, including the tour of the wholesale district on Fifth Avenue Uptown. "Amina, you may remember Saehan," he said. "He visited Damascus a few years back."

"I do." Amina turned to her husband. "Zacharias, with your experience in imports and exports, you may be interested in working in the wholesale district."

"I'm thinking the same," Zacharias said. "After the wedding we'll visit him. Sam, tell us more about Uniontown and New Salem."

"Uniontown is the county seat for Fayette County. The residents have gained their wealth from the coal mining industry."

"What's considered wealthy here?"

"J.V. Thompson, President of the First National Bank, owns most of the coal tract acreage along the Monongahela River. I've heard that he could sell his land for eighteen hundred dollars an acre. He's one of many millionaires in the city."

"I never thought the coal mining industry would be that lucrative. What do you think Thompson is worth?" Zacharias asked.

"About fifteen million. He's one of the investors who shop at our store— which is one reason we carry high-end ink pens, pocket watches, and perfumes." Sam pointed out the window. "We're approaching Uniontown. Look over that way and you can get a glimpse of the patch towns."

"Patch towns?"

"Those are the small towns that house the coal miners and their families."

Just at that second, the train pulled into the station. It was cold when they stepped down from the platform, but not snowing. *"Marhaba, Marhaba,"* Anthony and John greeted them. They'd been waiting for the train's arrival. "Sadie has prepared a welcome feast," Anthony said. "But first let's get you settled at the inn."

After loading the bags, everyone piled into the automobiles: Amina and Zacharias with Anthony, Sam and Anna with John.

"Zawhea, I'm so pleased to meet you," said John. "Sam's been counting the days. You'll enjoy your stay at the inn. The innkeeper and his wife are lovely people, and they'll make sure you're comfortable. Actually, everyone in New Salem is friendly and welcoming."

Sam smiled. *What John didn't say was that the entire town was talking about the arrival of his bride-to-be.*

"John, please call me Anna, my American name. Sam told me you and your wife came from Aleppo."

"Yes, we arrived five years ago. I've a feeling you and Elena will become fast friends."

At the New Salem Inn, Francis and Catherine Polanski, the innkeepers, were waiting at the front door. "Come in. Come in. We have the best rooms ready for you," Francis said. "Our living quarters are at the back of the check-in desk. So if you need anything, ring the bell. Since we run both the inn and the tavern, we're not always here at the front."

While Catherine showed her new guests to their rooms, John, Anthony, and Sam waited for them in the small parlor by the innkeeper's desk.

THE SYRIAN PEDDLER

Zacharias, Amina, and Anna took a few minutes to freshen up before they left for Sam's house and then on to Anthony's for dinner.

It was getting close to five o'clock by the time they drove away from the inn, so they were able to admire the Christmas decorations and lights as darkness fell.

John and Anthony dropped them off at Sam's. After he unlocked the door, Sam bowed and said, "Welcome to my home."

Without taking off her coat, Anna walked from room to room in a daze. *This is my new home. Wonder if I'll get used to this . . . so different. I feel like I'm in another world.* Sam followed her around. At the door of the bedroom, she stopped and turned to him. "This will be our room?"

"I hope it's to your liking, Anna."

"It's very nice. Will we have room for my babies?"

"I know you're sad without them. We'll move to a larger house."

"I'm sorry, Sam. I'm being selfish. I love the blue curtains and quilt. It's warm and comforting."

He took her hand. "Don't be sorry. Let me show you the kitchen. I've a few things, but I'm sure you'll want more."

She opened the cupboards and drawers. *He does have dishes and settings for four but, yes, we'll need more. And there's not much in the way of cooking pots. I hope we have money to stock the kitchen.*

Sam said, "I've been saving for your arrival. So you can shop for what you need. No worries."

Can he read my mind? "Yes, we should have more pots for cooking—and preparing dinners for company. We can shop together."

"Certainly. And soon."

"*Shukran,* Sam. You're a good and caring man. I'm beginning to feel better already. It'll simply take me time to adjust to this new land." Suddenly she thought of her future sister-in-law—another person who would be adjusting to America. "Where's Amina?" she asked.

Amina was standing by the bookcase. When Sam came into the room, she said, "You haven't lost your love for books. *The American Scene. The Book of Saint Albans. The Lighthouse at the End of the World.*"[1]

"Books—a real pleasure for me. Sit. Sit, everyone. Have some arak before we go to Anthony's."

"Brother, is that fresh pine I smell?" Amina asked.

112

Sam stopped pouring and looked toward the table. "Elena brought it over."

"What a delightful scent."

"Now a toast," said Sam.

Anna spoke up. "To my new home and my handsome Sam." She tipped her glass for a sip.

"I like that—Anna and Sam. I'm keeping Amina." "Well then, call me Zach."

The room overflowed with joyful laughter and love as they drank to their new lives.

After a while, Sam took Anna's hand. "It's time we leave for Anthony's. We'll take Maggie."

"Who's Maggie?" the three said in unison.

"My automobile."

"You named your automobile?" Amina asked.

"Why not? She was my favorite until Anna came back to me."

"Oh, Sam, you're funny," Anna said as she playfully ran her hands through his hair.

Tony opened the door and stood back to take in the new people. "*Umm,* Sam is here," he called.

Sadie approached the door, with Rima toddling behind. "I'm happy you arrived safely and in time for the holidays. Let me take your coats."

Anthony strode into the room. "I'll get them."

Tony looked from Amina to Anna as they took off their coats. Then he turned to Sam and said, "Which one is Zawhea?"

Smiling, Anna bent down to Tony's level and put her hand on his shoulder. "I'm Zawhea. That's my first name. And now I'd like to be called Anna, my middle name."

He looked her over. "You're pretty."

"Why, thank you. Sam tells me you have your own horse." "Did he tell you his name is Sammy?"

"Yes, and he told me it was your idea to call him Sam." "It was. 'Samuel' took too long to say."

"You're right. By the way, I'd like to see your horse sometime." "Now. Let's go now."

Sadie interrupted. "Tony, wait until it's daylight, and then you can ride your horse over to Sam's. Now, let's have mezza and *arak* everyone. Come to the living room."

Later, when Amina sat down at the table, she said, "Sadie, these aromas are a nostalgic mix—cinnamon, parsley, allspice. . . . I feel like I'm home. Don't you, Zach?"

"Our journey has just begun," Zach replied, taking Amina's hand.

Sadie had set her table with the finest lace cloth and dishes and had indeed prepared a fine feast—lentil soup, *tabbouleh* salad, baked *kibbeh* cabbage rolls, chicken, and rice pilaf.

Shortly after dinner, they gathered once again in the living room for *baklava* and *ahweh*. Soon Anna began to yawn. "It's been a long day."

"You must be tired. I'll wrap up some leftovers for you," Sadie said, heading to the kitchen.

As they were leaving, Anthony remarked to Sam, "Take the day off tomorrow and enjoy showing your family around the town."

When Sam pulled up at the inn, he told them, "I'll come get you in the morning—say, ten o'clock—for a drive to the nearby communities. After that, we'll meet the merchants in town."

Sam packed a bag with the fabric he had for Mrs. Benko, since he planned to stop by her farm. He backed Maggie out of the alley behind his house. *It's nice to have an automobile, but she can't take the place of a woman.*

After parking in front of the inn, he removed an item from the bag. Then he went to the front desk and found Catherine Polanski there. "Good morning. How are you this fine Friday?"

"I'm well, Sam. And you?"

"I'm one happy man today now that my family is here with me."

"They're happy too. I saw them after breakfast."

They both turned when they heard footsteps on the stairs.

It was Anna. When she reached the bottom, she said, "Zach and Amina are on their way down. How cold is it today?"

"You'll be warm enough in your long coat and boots. Let's sit in the parlor. I've a gift for you."

Anna admired the delicate white lace in the shape of a heart that hung from a dark blue cord. Then she unbuttoned her coat and slipped the pendant over her head. "I may never take it off. *Shukran.*"

"I knew you'd like it." He leaned in to give her a kiss.

"Good morning, you lovebirds," Amina said, smiling fondly as she entered the room. "We'd better set your wedding date soon."

"Let's go, and we can talk about the date on the way," Sam told her. *Having a big sister is a great help in times like this.*

Zach sat in front with Sam. Since the sun had come out, the snow was melting, making it easy driving on the snow-laden dirt roads.

The first farm they approached was the Benkos.' "I hope you get to meet Mary Benko," Sam told the others. "She's the best seamstress in town—and one of my favorite customers." He stopped in front of the frozen garden. "Wait here and I'll see if she's home."

When he knocked, he could hear one of the children crying. Mrs. Benko opened the door and said, "Sam, what a surprise. I didn't expect you today. Did your family arrive?"

"Yes, on Wednesday. We're driving around to see the neighboring communities and patch towns. So I brought your fabric."

"How kind of you. Do you have time for a short visit?"

"For you, Mrs. Benko, yes. I'll be right back with my family."

Mary Benko greeted the newcomers warmly. "Here you are, all the way from Syria. Sam was counting the days until you arrived. Come and sit. Coffee?"

Around the kitchen table, Anna, Amina, and Zach listened to stories of Mary Benko's family, her husband's work in the coal mine, and her sewing

When Anna heard her mention sewing, she said, "Sam told me about the lovely wedding gown you made for your daughter. Would you help me make my gown? I know we don't have much time."

"My dear, it would be such a pleasure. My husband and I were planning to go into town tomorrow morning. I could meet you at Abraham's to pick out a pattern and fabric. Around eleven, maybe?"

Anna's eyes shone with happiness. "Yes, tomorrow morning at eleven."

Later they drove from McClellandtown to Republic and Buffington and then back to New Salem to walk down Center Street and visit the shops. They ended at Abraham's Dry Goods, where Anna and Amina talked about patterns as the men discussed business.

"Amina, look at this pattern," said Anna. "It's for a simple yet elegant floor-length dress. And it's trimmed in lace, with a small bustle and long sheer sleeves. Actually, it's just what I had in mind for my wedding gown."

"It's perfect for your petite figure. Let's look at the fabrics."

Just as they began admiring the many selections, Sam walked over and said, "Zach and I are hungry. It's been a busy day. Let's all go eat at the tavern."

With the fire lit and lanterns on the tables, the tavern was warm and welcoming. Francis, always a gracious host, greeted them. "There's a corner table by the fireplace. Please sit. I'll bring you the bill of fare."

Sam pulled the chairs out for the ladies. "Catherine is one of the best cooks in the county," he commented.

"Sam, I heard that," Catherine said, coming up behind him. "Thank you. Francis told me you were here. My special this evening is shepherd's pie, made with lamb."

A smile spread across Sam's face. "My favorite, Catherine. You must have known we were coming."

Anna leaned toward Sam. "Is that what you're having?" He nodded. "It's delicious."

"I'll have the same," Anna remarked. Amina and Zach ordered the same. Fridays at the tavern were busy, since men dropped by after work to socialize, conduct business deals, and enjoy a pint. Before long, several people had stopped by their table to say hello and meet Sam's family.

After the food was served, Anna gingerly took a bite of the pie. "This is good. The flavor differs from our lamb stew. What do you think, Amina?"

"The demi-glace has wine, and it's missing a dab of cinnamon."

"That's it. It's the lack of cinnamon." Anna turned to Sam. "Do you eat here often?" She'd been thinking about this since they sat down. The bill of fare ranged from coffee and tea for five cents to the main courses for twenty-five cents.

"Every Friday," Sam replied. "It's hard to cook for one person. And I'm not the best."

I'm sure he's been lonely and likes the companionship here. Twenty-five cents isn't too much. What would that be in liras? I have to learn American dollars. Will he want to eat American dishes at home? I could learn from Catherine. Will I ever adjust to—

Sam interrupted her thoughts. "Anna, you're daydreaming. Tell me."

"Later, dear. It's only been three days."

Sam was with a customer when Anna arrived at the store the next morning. He glanced over and saw her looking at fabric with Mrs. Benko and Amina. *I wonder what she'll pick out. I wonder how she'll look on our wedding day.*

"Samuel, how much is this pocket watch?"

Sam turned his attention back to Ephraim, who he'd been helping. "Let me check the stock for you since this is our display piece. I'll be right back."

On his way to the stockroom he made a detour in the fabric aisle. "Good morning, my love," he whispered.

Anna turned and smiled.

21

That evening, while eating dinner, the four talked about wedding plans. "Father Salim stopped by the store this afternoon," Sam said. "He wants to meet with Anna and me tomorrow about a date. Anna, when do you think your gown will be ready?"

"By the eighteenth. Bless Mrs. Benko for agreeing to help. I'll cut out the pattern, and she'll do the sewing. Amina is designing the veil."

"I would marry you now in the dress you're wearing," Sam teased.

Zach glanced at his pocket calendar. "December twenty-first is a Saturday. How about that day?"

"Sounds good. Anna, the women of the parish have been waiting to meet you. Especially Mrs. Jawdy."

"Is she the one who tried to find you a wife?"

"Yes. And it wasn't just me, but all the other single men in town. We used to joke about it at the tavern."

Anna was the center of attention at the church coffee hour, and she seemed to enjoy it. Zach and Amina felt right at home as they talked with Sam's fellow parishioners.

Father Salim came over to them and said, "What a lovely family. I couldn't help but notice your beaming faces during the church service this morning. Have you thought about a wedding date?"

Sam replied, "We were wondering if you can perform the marriage on Saturday, December twenty-first."

"I'll need to check the calendar to be sure. Please bring your family into my office. Then we can finalize the plans."

When the four of them entered his office, Father said, "Have a seat. And, to the newcomers, welcome to New Salem. I hope you've rested up from the long voyage. You'll find New Salem a very friendly place—different from the larger cities, where immigrants tend to live in their own communities. In fact, my first parish assignment was in the Brooklyn community of South Ferry, called Little Syria. I believe Anthony has friends there."

"Yes, Father," Sam said. "The Nadars. I stayed with them just last week. So how does your calendar look?"

"Ah, yes. Back to the wedding. December twenty-first is good. At noon? You can rehearse late Friday afternoon in the church."

Anna smiled. "Father Salim, this is perfect."

The next two weeks were a flurry of activity. Sam and Zach worked in the store or else were on the road taking orders and making deliveries. They met Anna and Amina each evening for dinner at Sam's home. There, they caught up on how plans were progressing for the wedding and the Christmas holiday.

On one of those evenings, Anna told Sam, "Amina and I had coffee with Sadie and Elena. They're helping us with the preparations."

Then a week before the wedding, Anna, Amina, Elena, and Sadie were in the church hall making final decisions for the reception.

Elena said, "Let's think about the food. Many of the women have offered to bake a dish or dessert—and not just the women from St. George's. Don't you think we should have more than our Syrian dishes?"

Amina looked at her journal. "I have a list of what the ladies from St. George's offered to make. Anna has a list that Mrs. Benko gave her from the ladies in the Catholic Church."

"I'll combine the lists. Then we can review the final menu after church tomorrow," Sadie said.

"Wonderful," Anna said. "What would I do without each of you? All I can think about is finishing my gown. We only have to add the sleeves to the bodice and then sew the bodice to the skirt. I've already finished sewing the lace and beads onto the bodice." She turned to Amina. "And how is the veil coming along?"

"You'll have to look at it when we get back to the inn this afternoon. And I want you to try it on before I finish."

Later, when the two of them were in Anna's room, Amina placed the lace headpiece on Anna and then attached the tulle with bobby pins. They both looked in the mirror, teary-eyed, as they combed Anna's hair around her face. The veil was like her gown, simple but elegant with ecru lace sewn to a round crown, and white tulle attached in three layers. The first was halfway down Anna's back, the second midway, and the third to her neckline. She turned to hug Amina. "Soon we'll be sisters-in law. The veil is beautiful. I feel like a bride, and this time I'm ready to be one."

"The first marriage was difficult, I know. I'm fortunate that Zach and I knew each other before our marriage."

"Will you two have dinner with us tonight?"

"No. We're going to eat here in the tavern. You and Sam should have some time alone. We've been eating dinner together ever since we arrived. After all, the wedding is a week from today."

Anna giggled like a little girl. "Amina, you know I've been counting every day, hour, and minute."

"Just tell me what the front of your dress looks like. Have you attached the lace?"

"Sam, you know I want to surprise you. And, yes, I've finished the lace and added pearl buttons. Monday I'm going to Mrs. Benko's for the final fitting. . . . She wants me to call her Mary. I find it hard to do."

"I do too. It's because of the respect we have for people the same age as our parents. Mrs. Benko is like a mother to many of us. She and her husband have been wonderful, kind customers. Her daughter's wedding was a year ago this month. I never imagined then that I'd be marrying you a year later. . . . Well, I did dream that it would happen someday."

"To think she's making my gown just a year later. One day we'll have a big happy family like the Benkos. By the way, has your suit arrived?"

"No. It was to have been delivered to the store today. So were our wedding bands. If they don't arrive on Monday, I'll telegraph Saehan."

After dinner, they washed the dishes together then went to the parlor, where Sam played his darbuka and Anna read *The American Scene*. She didn't notice that Sam had stopped playing until he lifted the book from her hands and bent over to kiss her. She kissed him back then said, "It's time I walk back to the inn. We only have one week to wait."

"Yes. Let's get our coats."

Outside the inn, despite the cold of the night, they both found it very hard to say goodbye.

Sunday after church, Zach, Sam, and Anthony walked to the store to make certain all the Christmas orders were ready. They also wanted to schedule deliveries for those customers who couldn't get to the store to pick them up.

The women stayed in the church hall to discuss the food lists Sadie had combined. Margaret and Tony were drawing with their crayons at a nearby table. Anna was holding Rima.

Elena commented on the list. "I think we need a few more desserts. So I'll bake several pans of *baklava*.

"I'll help you," Amina said.

They finalized the menu and went on to talk about decorating the church pews with white organza and pine boughs. Elena would cut the organza and tie the material into bows. There were plenty of pine trees in the countryside.

"Tony will help me cut the pine," Sadie said.

Hearing his name, Tony came over to his mother. "What will I do?" "You and Margaret can help me cut pine for Anna's wedding."

Tony went running back to the table, shouting, "We're going to cut pine boughs for Sam's wedding."

Monday morning Amina knocked on Anna's door. "Are you ready to go to Mrs. Benko's?" she asked. "Zach is here with Sam's automobile to take us."

"Come in. I'll only be a minute."

"Why, you're flitting around like a little bird. A lovebird."

"I can't find my white stockings, and my shoes are still at the store." "You don't need your stockings today. And we'll stop and get your shoes." Anna sat on the bed. *I'm falling apart. Can't think straight. It's all happening so fast.* "I'm not sure I can go today," she told Amina.

"Anna, you must. Mrs. Benko is expecting us for your final fitting. Come now. You'll be fine."

"Amina, what would I do without you?"

22

Early in the morning, Anthony and John were setting up the tables and chairs in the hall. After Sadie, Elena, Margaret, and Tony finished tying the bows and pine on the ends of the church pews, they went to the hall to lay white linens on the tables and add a few pine boughs for centerpieces. As they walked in, men were playing their darbukas, practicing for the wedding dances.

"Are we ready?" Sadie asked.

Elena nodded and grinned.

While Amina was in Anna's room, where they were dressing, Zach was at Sam's house.

"Help. I can't get this tie right," Sam shouted. "Zach, where are you?" *What's going on with me?*

"Here in the kitchen," Zach called. "You sound crazy, man. Calm down. I'll be right there."

Sam was sitting on the bed with his shirt out of his trousers and his tie still undone when Zach walked in.

"We have twenty minutes before we need to be at the church," his brother-in-law told him. "Let me help you with that tie."

Sam tucked the shirt in, put on his vest and suit jacket, and took a deep breath. "I'm ready. Let's go. You better drive. I'm too nervous."

At the inn, Catherine softly called upstairs, "John is here for you lovely ladies."

Anna and Amina had just finished putting on jewelry, the pendants Sam had given them. Anna also wore a blue cameo necklace her mother had given her. Amina carried Anna's veil as they walked down the stairs.

"Oh, look at you!" Catherine exclaimed. "Beautiful. Just beautiful. Now, you get on to the church before I start to cry. Francis and I have closed the inn and will leave in a minute."

The bodice of the gown had a lace insert decorated with tiny pearl buttons, and the rest of it was thin cotton, with embroidered flowers that continued down the long sleeves. The organza skirt flowed in an A-line down to her ankles, showing a bit of white stocking and the tips of her ecru shoes with pointed toes. It was a perfect picture of a gorgeous and happy bride-to-be.

The snow glistened under the noon sun as friends entered the church. The pews were soon full, and music was playing as everyone waited for the ceremony to begin.

Tony was trying to sit still and be quiet. Every minute or two, he turned around to look behind him. "Where's Sam? When will he be here with Anna?" "You'll see them come in from the back of the church with Father Salim,"
Sadie told him. "Please stop squirming."
The musicians stopped playing for the wedding party to enter. Father Salim walked ahead, followed by Sam and Anna, Amina, and Zach, who was the Koumbaro or sponsor.
Once they reached the altar, Father began the blessing of the rings. He blessed the bride and groom three times with the rings to signify their lives entwined into one, then placed them on the ring fingers of their right hands. Zach exchanged the rings three times on their fingers as a symbol of their strength as a married couple.
Lifting the crowns from the altar, Father blessed them, then placed them upon Sam's and Anna's heads, chanting, "O Lord our God, crown them with glory and honor." Zach exchanged the crowns over their heads to seal the union. The couple smiled with tears in their eyes as they watched Zach.
Father blessed the wine in the common cup, offering it up as a sign of their shared life. Then he led them around an altar table placed in front of the pews to celebrate the union, while the guests joined in the Orthodox wedding chants.
He turned to face Sam and said, "Be magnified, O Bridegroom, as Abraham, and blessed as Isaac, and increased as was Jacob. Go your way in peace, performing in righteousness the commandments of God."

Then to Anna he said, "And you, O Bride, be magnified as was Sarah, and rejoiced as was Rebecca, and increased as Rachel, being glad in your husband, keeping the paths of the Law, for so God is well pleased."

Removing their crowns, he continued, "Accept the crowns of the now Mr. and Mrs. Samuel Hanna in Your Kingdom unsoiled and undefiled; and preserve them without offense to the ages of ages."

Sam embraced Anna, whispering, "Your gown is as beautiful as you are"—and then they turned smiling as they waited at the altar, where friends came to congratulate them.

As the guests left the church, the talk among the women was all about Anna's gown. "You've sewn two beautiful gowns in a year," one of them told Mary Benko.

"The gowns are only as beautiful as the fabric and lace sold at Anthony and Sam's store," she replied. "And Anna attached the lace and the pearl buttons. She's a talented young woman."

"And the veil?" another asked.

"Amina designed it. A perfect touch. She and Anna are like daughters to me—as if I needed more children." Mary Benko laughed.

All the guests were in the church hall mingling and eating mezza when Zach and Amina entered the reception, followed by Sam and Anna. Everyone stood up and clapped. Anthony started the traditional dance music, and the celebration began. Most of the guests joined in to dance the *Al-Shamaliyya*. Tony and Margaret led the other children in one circle hopping around to their own version.

After several dances, Zach went to the front of the room and stopped the music. "Time to toast," he announced. He waited until everyone had found a seat and had a glass in their hand.

"Sam and Anna, may you have love and joy in your marriage. May friends and family forever surround you. May your work be blessed with success. To Mr. and Mrs. Samuel Hanna."

While everyone stood and raised their glasses, saying "To Sam and Anna," Tony went up to Zach. "I've a toast," he said.

"Tony has a toast," Zach told the guests.

"Sam has been my big brother for a long time. He won't be lonely anymore. Anna is here—and she's pretty."

Sam and Anna got up to hug Zach and Tony then continued standing. Sam turned to the guests. "Thank you, my friends, for sharing this glorious time with us. You welcomed me into this community, and now Anna. To my beautiful wife, welcome to your new home. Friends, please enjoy the food, music, and dancing."

Later, as they were eating, Anna remarked, "Look around us. We have a blend of cultures—yet we're all friends. I love this, you—and America."

"My dear, I agree. We'll have a wonderful life here together." He lowered his voice. "Can we leave soon? I want to be alone with you."

"Why, we can't leave yet. There's dessert and more dancing. Our friends and family want to celebrate with us."

Just then, Anthony picked up Anna and twirled her around, while the men grabbed Sam and started another dance. They danced and sang through the afternoon and early evening with good food, drink, and love.

Finally, the bride and groom felt comfortable enough to say their goodbyes. After many hugs and kisses, they were able to leave the church hall. Sam paused just outside the door and put his arms around Anna for a long kiss. Snowflakes were falling, lightly resting on their eyelashes. There they stood together, under a December moon that looked like a painting hung in the sky.

23

"Finally alone with my wife," Sam said.

"I thought I loved you as a young girl—in the only way I knew," Anna told him. "I talked to my first husband just once before we married. I found it very difficult to be in an arranged marriage to a man I didn't know."

They snuggled together under the warm covers in Sam's bed—now their bed—and continued to talk about the wedding between passionate kisses. He caressed her shoulders and slowly untied the bodice of her ribbon-laced nightgown—his desire burning.

The morning sun peeped through the curtains, and the snow had stopped falling.

They began to kiss as he murmured, "I can't stop touching you. Your skin is softer than I imagined—and so smooth. Like silk. Anna, we're made for each other. . . . I'm having trouble finding the right words to explain how deep my love is for you."

They eventually got out of bed, cooked breakfast, and spent the day at home talking about plans for the future and Sam's desire to have his own store.

"I can help at Abraham's until we've saved enough to open our own," Anna offered.

"Only if you want to. . . . You know, I'd love to stay home with you tomorrow, but I have to go to work."

"I understand. You'll have time off after the holidays. And I've much to do here at home this week."

Shortly after the store opened on Monday, the aisles were bustling with customers. Zach and Amina had left to find a home in Pittsburgh. Anna began to prepare for Christmas—shopping, baking, and adding a woman's touch to their home.

One day after work, Sam walked in the front door, took a deep breath, and shouted, "Fresh Syrian bread. How I've missed that smell. Many times I pictured you here baking."

Anna laughed and grabbed Sam by the waist as he bent over the table and tore off a piece. "No more until dinner."

"You're scolding me," he said sheepishly. He took off his tie and sat down at the table. "Tell me what you want for Christmas. I've yet to shop."

"I miss the bright silk fabrics in Damascus. I'd love to have some to sew a few frocks with."

"You don't have to make your clothing. We'll buy your frocks in Uniontown or Pittsburgh."

"Sam, I enjoy sewing. . . . There are some things you don't know about me yet."

He looked deeply into her eyes. "Yes, there are."

"Mary Benko said I could use her machine. By the way, I have an idea for a gift for you."

"You can use her machine for a time, but then you should have your own. My gift—will you buy it at our store?"

"You *are* a tease. What do you think about inviting the Abrahams and Nazzifs for Christmas dinner?"

"Yes. Let's do that."

"It'll also be a farewell dinner for Zach and Amina. Oh, how I'll miss them."

Sam touched Anna's cheek. "They won't be far away. With the train, a visit will be easy. Don't worry, my dear."

The next day Anna stopped by the store. She went to the back to look for Sadie. "I'm buying Sam a pocket watch," Anna told her. "It's the third gold one from the left in the watch counter. When you can, would you take it out and put it in a safe place for me? And please make sure he doesn't see you." She reached into her reticule. "I think this is the right amount. If it isn't, let me know when I come to pick it up tomorrow."

"I can drop it by your house in the morning," Sadie told her.

"Wonderful. See you then."

The next day, Sadie knocked on the door while Anna was setting up the manger—the nativity crib—in the parlor. A chill swept through the house when Sadie came in. "It's cold this morning. Hurry in," Anna told her friend.

The two women sat down at the kitchen table. Sadie put Rima on the floor. It didn't take her long to crawl over and explore the manger.

"Sadie, coffee or tea?"

"Coffee. Here. I've brought the watch. Sam has been looking intently at the pocket watches. They're a popular gift this Christmas."

"He'll be happy and surprised." She examined the watch then put it down. "Sam and I would love for you and your family to come for Christmas dinner."

"What a nice idea. An early dinner would be best for the children."

"I was thinking the same. We're going to invite John and his family, and of course Amina and Zach will be back. Are you ready for the holiday?"

"I still have some baking to do, and Anthony wants me to stop by the store this afternoon to go over the books. . . . Oh, Anna, I don't know what we'd do without Sam. One day he'll have his own store. I hope by then Tony will be old enough to work after school."

"A store. That's his dream—and mine."

"Why, you have tears in your eyes. Is something wrong?"

Anna stifled a sob. "I want a family more than a store. And I wonder when that will happen. I miss my babies back home—but now I'm here with Samuel. Am I selfish, do you think?" She wiped away the tears.

"You're not selfish. Enjoy your time without children for the moment. They'll come. Relax. You'll see."

Rima had crawled to the kitchen and was looking at Anna with her big eyes. Anna laughed as she picked her up. "Come here, little one."

"Do you want to come over tomorrow and bake shortbread?" Sadie asked. "Tony's going to help in the store now that school is on break. We need to keep him busy. He's so excited about Papa Noel."

"I'll bring some flour and trimmings. What time?"

"Is ten o'clock good?"

"Perfect."

Sadie lifted Rima from Anna's lap. "Come, Rima. It's time to go. We have shopping to do."

Amina and Zach had arrived back at the inn the day before Christmas. Anna stopped by with her arms full of groceries. "Catherine, have you seen Amina?" she asked the innkeeper.

"They just left. I think Zach was going to help in the store. And Amina said she was going to your home."

"How did I miss them on my way here? I'm excited to hear if they found a place."

"They did. Amina told me all about it. Hurry on to catch up with her. Merry Christmas, dear."

As Anna approached her house, she saw Amina sitting on the front step. She called out, "There you are. I was just at the inn."

"Hand me the groceries so you can unlock the door. I'm freezing." "It's unlocked."

"Remember what Sam told us about the robbery? Don't you think you should lock up when you leave?"

They went inside, and Anna put the groceries on the table. "You're right. From now on I'll take more care. Let's talk while I put the food away. I'm baking lamb for tomorrow. The Abrahams and Nazzifs are joining us for Christmas dinner."

"What a nice way to celebrate the holiday—with friends and family." "Tea, while you tell me about your time in Pittsburgh?"

"Yes, please. To warm me up. We stayed in a boarding house near Saehan and his family. They're in a Syrian community. Zach met several of Saehan's friends who work in wholesale, and one of them offered him a job. When we move next week, we'll stay in the boarding house until we see if we like the city."

"You'll like it, being used to city life. Of course, the cities here are nothing like at home. But, then, America is young." She paused. "I miss the majesty of our churches and the ancient history that's a part of our country. It's an undeniable quality of our lives. Don't you agree?"

"Certainly. It's going to take us a long time to become accustomed to the American ways. But you're happy, aren't you, Anna?"

"I truly am, even if I miss our beautiful Damascus." She glanced at the clock. "Look at the time. I have to start preparing the food."

"I'll stay and help you."

"Wonderful. Oh, I'll miss you so when you move."

Sam woke early on Christmas morning and rolled over. "Anna, are you awake?"

She sat up quickly. "What is it? Is something wrong?" "Not at all, dear. Papa Noel is here. Merry Christmas." "Our first Christmas as husband and wife."

They went to the kitchen to make coffee. Sam couldn't wait any longer.

"Open it," he said, holding out her present.

"Blue and green silks. I love these colors. And lace, ribbons, thread. What beautiful clothes I'll make." She leaned over to kiss him.

"Anna, tucked in the blue fabric you'll find something." Unrolling it, she discovered a silver band with a small stone in the center.

"My favorite stone—turquoise." A tear or two dotted her cheek as she slipped the ring onto her finger. "Samuel, you're too good to me."

"Dear, nothing is too good for you."

"*Shukran.*" Now, open this gift."

He took the object from the box. "I've been admiring the pocket watches in the store, including this one. I remember seeing my father take his out and thinking, 'One day I'll have a watch exactly like his.' How did you know?"

"I didn't know. I just thought you'd like it."

"It's beautiful. Thank you," he said while kissing her.

After church, Anna and Amina were in the kitchen preparing dinner and singing to the music their husbands were playing. When the lamb, kibbeh and cabbage rolls were in the oven, they joined the men in the parlor.

Zach stopped playing the oud. "You two look like sisters—from your beautiful dark eyes, to your smiles, and to how you wear your hair. Aren't we the lucky men?"

"We're sisters in spirit too," Anna said as she picked up a gift from the table. "Here, sis. This is for you."

"You made this, didn't you?" Amina asked, holding up a scarf that was green as a pine bough and trimmed with white lace. She wrapped it over her shoulders, stood up, and twirled around. "When did you find the time?"

"While you were in Pittsburgh, I was able to use Mrs. Benko's machine."

"I love it. Merry Christmas." Amina handed Anna a package. "Zach and I found this in Pittsburgh. I don't think you have one." "What could it be?"

"Something for my automobile?" Sam asked.

Anna removed the wrapping. "I'm happy you have Maggie, my dear, but I hope it's for our home." It was—an ecru lace tablecloth. "Amina, it's perfect for our table. I love the intricate design. Come. Let's put it on right now."

Sam began strumming his darbuka. "Zach," he said, "time for arak and more music."

Soon it was five o'clock and the other guests arrived. Sadie brought desserts. Elena had Syrian bread, fresh from the oven.

"Merry Christmas!" Anna exclaimed as she took their coats.

Tony and Margaret were soon sitting on the floor with their favorite gifts, and Rima was toddling around them. The adults enjoyed mezza and drinks while waiting for dinner to finish cooking. Anna sat next to Sam thinking what a joy it was to have friends in their home on this special holiday.

The next morning Anna woke early. She shook Sam awake and said, "We should get dressed and go to the inn. Amina and Zach will be leaving soon for Pittsburgh."

"Yes, let's dress and drive over . . . have breakfast with them there."

An hour later, Amina and Anna had a tearful goodbye.

"It was a wonderful Christmas," said Amina, "having dinner with you, Sam, and our friends here in New Salem. Please write often. I'll miss you."

"I will—and you too," Anna said as she hugged Amina.

24

One February afternoon Sadie went into the back office to find Anna there, crying. "What's wrong?" she asked.

"It's nothing. . . . Yes, it is something," Anna replied. "I'm beginning to wonder if I can have another baby. Samuel and I keep trying and nothing happens."

"Oh dear. You know, I tried for several years after Tony, and then came Rima. Try to relax and enjoy your time together." Sadie hugged her and said, "One never knows when it will happen."

"Please don't tell Samuel you saw me in tears. I don't want him to worry." "I'll not say anything to him or to Anthony."

"I know you won't. To keep my mind off it, I've been thinking about becoming more involved in our church. Maybe we could start a ladies group to help those in need. I've seen some of the families struggle—especially after the loss of a husband or son in the mines. What do you think?"

"That's an idea. Let's talk to Father Salim about it."

The following Tuesday Anna and Sadie were in Father Salim's office to talk about their plan.

"Well, our parish has grown to the point that we're able to give more to others," Father said. "Why don't you ask other women to join a—a Ladies Society. Yes, that's what we'll call the group. You have my blessings."

"*Shukran*, Father," Anna and Sadie said together.

Over dinner that evening Anna told Sam about her day. "Sadie and I met with Father Salim. With his blessing, we're going to begin a women's group in the church to donate time and goods to help needy people. I think about those coal miners who've died and left their families with so little, and I know I can do something for them."

"My dear, you've only been here two months," Sam said, "yet you've already made so many friends—and now you want to help our neighbors and community. I'm proud of you."

"I wasn't prepared for the suffering the coal miners experience. My heart goes out to them. Imagine the young children left without a father. I've begun to let other women know about the group. We plan to meet in the church hall soon."

A week later Sadie and Anna were surprised at how many women showed up for the first meeting. It was a cold winter day, yet they came with their babies and younger children. Over coffee and tea, the women organized themselves into groups. Some would collect clothes, some would sort them, and others would deliver them.

Winter turned to spring as the St. George's Ladies Society worked to help many families with food and clothing donations. By early summer the society was well known throughout Fayette County.

It was a warm June day when Anna walked into the house after delivering clothing. Feeling nauseous, she sat down, rubbed her stomach, smiled, and said a prayer.

Sam came home from work to find her in bed. *Anna, asleep at dinnertime?* He quietly went to the kitchen and sat down to read the paper. He was still at the table when she walked into the room. "Samuel, what are you doing here?" she asked. "It's six o'clock, my dear."

"I must have been exhausted to have slept for two hours." "I was worried you were ill."

"No, just tired. Elena and I dropped some clothes by Dr. Eckerd's office. He'll take them to Cottage State Hospital. He told us nine men were injured in the Ronco mine last week and that five were being discharged tomorrow." She turned toward the stove. "I'll heat up the rice and *malfouf* and we can eat soon."

"Our customers have been telling me about the good your Society is doing for the community. Come here."

She sat on his lap and hugged him. "It makes me feel good to help." She let out a long sigh. "Today I feel fatigued for some reason."

Anna walked into the store and said, "Anthony, is Samuel here?" "He should be back shortly. You sound in a rush."

"I am. I'll just wait if you don't mind."

"Make yourself at home. It's rather slow this afternoon."

A few minutes later, in walked Mrs. Jawdy. "Anthony, I'm looking for a pair of dress shoes in size eight," she said. "Preferably in black."

The minute Anna heard that voice, out the door she went, and as fast as possible. *That woman saw me walk out of the doctor's office. I can do without such a busybody in my life. Ah, it comes with a small town—the gossip.*

"Anna, where are you off to?" Sam called, walking out of the barbershop. "I came to see if you were at the store. I was going to wait for you—until Mrs. Busybody arrived."

Sam smiled. "Oh. That must be our friend, Mrs. Jawdy." "Do you have a minute to talk?" "Of course. Are you all right?"

"No. Well, yes—I think." Even though they were in the middle of Center Street, in the middle of a workday, Anna blurted out, "We're having a baby."

"A what? A baby?"

"Yes, Samuel. A baby."

He picked her up, swirled her around, and put her down on the sidewalk.

He let out a holler. "I'm going to be a father!" Then he told her, "Wait here."

Anna watched him run into the store and, soon after that, walk nonchalantly out the door to where she was waiting.

"Let's go home," he told her, "and then I want to hear all about this." As they walked, Sam related the conversation he'd had with Anthony.

"Mrs. Jawdy was still there, so I asked Anthony to take a minute so I could show him the latest bank report. We went to the back of the store so she couldn't hear us. I told him our good news and asked for the afternoon off.

He sends you his best. . . . Oh, I asked him not to tell anyone. Except Sadie, of course."

Anna stood on her tiptoes to kiss him. "Thank you."

When they were at the kitchen table, Anna explained, "The last month or so, I've been feeling sick in the morning and tired in the late afternoon. This afternoon I went to visit Dr. Eckerd. He confirmed that I'm healthy and going to have a baby. I haven't told you how much I've been wanting this—a child with you. Are you happy?"

"Full of joy—and more. I don't have the words to express my feelings at this moment. There's enough space in our bedroom for a crib, but we'll look for a larger home. My prayer is that we have many more children together."

"Oh, Samuel, my love, this is the best news." She hugged him. "I'll be seeing the doctor on a regular basis. He suggests I deliver the baby in the Uniontown Hospital. These days it's the safest thing to do, although he is still delivering many babies at home. . . . I didn't realize the hospital has only been open for five years."

"I haven't had to even think of the hospital until now. We want the best care for you and our babies." He gave her a kiss. "Let's walk over to John and Elena's to tell them. He'll be home from the shop by now."

That evening, back home and still glowing from the warm congratulations given by their friends, Anna wrote to her parents and Amina, while Sam wrote to his parents with the good news.

The months prior to the baby's birth were exciting times and sad times. Sad, as there was a shootout between several Italian and Slavic men at the Ronco mines. Two were killed in the fracas. Such violence among nationalities in the small community was a shock. Sure—there had been disputes, many friendly in nature, but this was different. Then news arrived of the sinking of the S.S. *Neustria* in October of 1908 as it sailed from New York to Marseilles. Sam and Anna read the story on the front page of the Uniontown papers. They felt sad, but grateful there were no passengers on board—only thirty-eight crewmembers. The *Neustria*, built in 1883, had sailed between continents for twenty-five years, and Sam, Anna, and many of their friends had arrived in America on the ship.

It was an exciting time as Anna went through her pregnancy almost problem-free. The months passed by quickly.

That Christmas Amina and Zach sent word they would visit. Sam had seen them only once since they moved to Pittsburgh—when he was on a buying trip. Anna, not having seen them at all, had been counting the days to their arrival, since she dearly missed her friend.

The day finally came. Amina rushed up the front steps, arms full of parcels. Anna had been peering out the window waiting. Amidst the hugs, they couldn't stop talking.

"Where's Zach?" Anna finally asked.

"Outside discussing automobiles with Sam. He wants advice on buying one."

"He's asking the right man. Heaven knows where he learned it all."

"Look at you, glowing, and getting bigger. Have you chosen names?" "We agreed on John Ellien if it's a boy and Mary if it's a girl. . . . And look at *you*. You're as beautiful as ever. Let's sit down in the kitchen, and you can tell me about city life."

"Our lives revolve around church and friends. And the city itself? It offers more hustle and bustle. Walking to the different shops and street stands is entertaining, and you see a lot of peddlers around. There doesn't seem to be much prejudice. . . . Remember our first day in Manhattan? Being called black? I was so afraid."

"So was I. But Samuel stayed calm. He later told me the entire story of the first time he was called black, and how he lost his temper. You know, he sees no color in people—just *them*—and he tries to be kind to everyone."

"That's my brother. Yet he does have a temper at times when there's, how they say, a bump in the road. . . . By the way, how is Mary Benko?"

"Mary is the same loving mother. She finally convinced me to call her by her first name. She asks about you every time I see her. I admire that she never gossips like some of the other women. . . . Speaking of gossips, Mrs. Jawdy saw me coming out of the doctor's office when I found out I was pregnant. Soon the women were asking me if I was sick. Of course, they know I take donations to Dr. Eckerd for the miners, so who knows what she told her friends. I'm still getting used to living in a small community."

"Word travels fast. Actually, I see the same thing in our Syrian community, although there are many more people. It surprised me to learn that Pittsburgh is becoming one of the largest cities in America. A melting pot it is." Amina touched Anna's hand. "Like you, I've become active in our church, and that helps in making friends. I must admit, though, I don't make friends as easily as you, Anna. Oh, I miss our talks and times together."

"Me too. In your last letter you said you wanted to tell me something when we next saw each other. I've been concerned ever since. What is it?"

Amina got up and walked to the kitchen sink. "Yes, I didn't want to write you about—about the miscarriage that had happened a week earlier. I wasn't ill afterward, just sad. I didn't tell Zach, so please don't say anything. We've been trying and trying."

Going to Amina's side, Anna wrapped her arms around her sister-in-law's shoulders. "I'm so sorry. Did you see a doctor?"

"I saw Dr. Huffman, who delivers at Shadyside Hospital. He sees no reason I can't bear children. He advised me to relax and try not to worry. To keep my mind occupied, I've started teaching English to the women in our neighborhood who want to learn. Many of them speak only Arabic. . . . And I've made a few friends along the way."

"Amina, it's hard not to focus on your loss. But I've a feeling you'll soon be pregnant again. For now, I'm happy we're together."

Later that evening, the four headed to the tavern, where they reminisced about the past year—the voyage, the wedding, and last Christmas.

"Elena is having us for dinner this year. Sam, what shall we make?" Anna said.

"You should rest more. I'll make *malfouf*, and we'll bring arak."

Anna looked at him and smiled. *This second Christmas with Sam is better than the first. We're having a baby and celebrating again with family and friends . . .*

Sam had surprised Anna with a sewing machine. After the New Year, the machine and fabric became her passion as she began sewing an A-line skirt—and not just any skirt. This one was pale green with light blue ribbon trimming down the sides to the hem, and then she applied lace to the hem— a cheery addition to her wardrobe for after the baby's arrival.

25

"Sam. Sam, Wake up. I'm in labor. We should go to the hospital." Sam rubbed his eyes and rolled over. "What did you say?"

"Labor. Hospital. Samuel, it's time."

He jumped out of bed and ran to the wardrobe to find clothes. "Where's your bag? Where is it, Anna?"

Several hours later, Sam paced the waiting area while Anna was in delivery. He was relieved that Dr. Eckerd happened to be on call, since Doc was a trusted friend.

Mid-morning, Doc walked up to him with the announcement. "Sam, come meet your son. Anna delivered a healthy boy and is doing well."

There he was, a chubby baby with a swath of dark hair. Sam had tears in his eyes as he bent over to kiss Anna and look intently at his first child.

"My dear husband, meet our son," she said.

The proud, beaming father that he was spent the afternoon handing out cigars to the merchants in town. Then, after visiting Anna again in the late afternoon, he went to the carpenter shop. He and John talked as they worked to finish the baby's cradle.

"I never thought about how one learns to be a father until today," Sam said. "Now I *am* one, and I pray I'll know what to do. I think back to my first year here—being called black, the anger, and the robbery. I hope my children don't experience the same."

John responded, "We do the best we can and continue to pray. In the meantime, we experience the joy in our lives."

"True. You know, Anna and I would like you and Elena to be our first son's godparents."

"We'll be honored. And now, if you don't have plans for dinner, come join us."

"Nothing I'd like better tonight."

The day Anna brought John home from the hospital, she and Sam stood holding hands, looking at their baby sleeping in the cradle. Then the cries began.

"What do we do?" Sam looked puzzled as she watched Anna pick up John and rock him.

"He's probably crying because he's hungry." "I do have a lot to learn about babies."

And Sam did learn, since the future held many more additions to their family.

Two weeks later, John Ellien Hanna, born on March 9, 1909, was baptized with his godparents at his side. John grew quickly, with much love around him. Tony, Margaret, and Rima wanted to hold him, read to him, and carry him around—he was like the new baby doll in town. Sam had returned to work, and Anna was thrilled to be a mother once again.

Many visitors stopped by to see the baby. Mary Benko was among the first. "What a precious child," she told Anna. "I've brought you something. It's my favorite to read to little ones."

"What a lovely book. And the illustration are beautiful." Anna flipped through the pages of *Mother Goose in Prose*. "Thank you."

"I remember reading it to my first-born like it was yesterday."

"Mary, you've been like a mother to me. I feel blessed with your friendship and able advice. Tell me how your family is, since I haven't been to visit for a few months."

"Everyone is good. My little ones are growing so quickly that soon they'll be on their own. Then I'll have grandbabies. The youngest are shopping with their father now. You know, we come to town every other Saturday. When we come next, I'd be happy to stay with John. You could have time to shop alone. I know what it's like to do errands with a little one."

"If you wouldn't mind, how about the next Saturday you're here? I must admit, it would be nice to go shopping without the baby. You know the time it takes to select fabric, and he becomes fussy if we're out too long."

"Yes, my dear. I'll come in the early afternoon."

After Mary left, Anna put John down for a nap and took the time to write a letter to her family in Syria.

THE SYRIAN PEDDLER

April 20, 1909
Dear Abb and Umm,

We had our first baby, John Ellien, on March 9. He looks like Samuel, with his dark curly hair and deep brown eyes. What a joy to have a baby once more—and with Samuel.

Please write more and tell me all about Mitelj and Martha. I miss them. We are saving to buy their tickets as soon as they are old enough to travel alone.

Have you seen Samuel's parents lately? Please give them my love Amina and Zach were here for Christmas. They like living in Pittsburgh. We will see them again soon. The train is direct to Uniontown, so it is an easy trip.

I hope you are in good health.
Inshallah,
Anna

It wasn't long before she heard John's whimpering. *Perfect timing.* She sealed the envelope. Then she fed and dressed him to go mail the letter and check the post. They walked to town, stopping to say hello whenever friends wanted to take a peek at John, wrapped in a blanket in the baby carriage

There was a letter from Amina in the afternoon post. Anna put it in her pocket and headed back home after one stop at the grocer's. Later, while dinner was in the oven, she sat down to read it.

April 10, 1909
Dear Anna,

How is baby John? I am dying to see him. Zach and I are talking about a visit in early summer—when he will be able to take a few days off work. He has been so busy.

Now, sit down if you are not already sitting. I am going to have a baby in October. You can imagine how happy we are. I am three months now, and Dr. Huffman says all goes well so far. I have a good feeling about this one. Pray for me. Oh, I wish I could have shared this news with you next to me. Please write soon.
My love,
Amina

Anna held the letter to her bosom and sighed just as Sam walked in the door.

"Sam, Amina's having a baby in October. I just finished reading her letter. Here. You read it."

"Wonderful news!" Sam exclaimed. "I'm happy for her and Zach. John will have a close cousin." He gave her a broad smile. "When shall we try for another baby, darling?"

She kissed him. "Let's wait a while. John is only a month old. Hear him now?"

Sam picked up John as Anna put dinner on the table.

26

The Hanna family grew, and Sam continued to save for his store. John was two when Anthony, named after Anthony Abraham, was born. In 1913, Mary, named after Mary Benko, followed. When she turned a year old, the family moved to a larger house still within walking distance of Abraham's Dry Goods.

Soon after they were settled in the new home, Anna became pregnant with their fourth child. In the spring of 1915, their second baby girl arrived. They named her Anna but called her Honey. The boys shared a room, as did the girls. They were active, healthy children growing up in a loving environment.

"Anna, I'm home," Sam called over the banter of the four children. Today Mary was trying to help her mother bake bread. She picked up the dough and turned it over, nearly dropping it on the floor. The boys were teasing Honey, who was trying to crawl across the kitchen.

"John and Tony, what are you doing home from school?" Sam asked. "We only had a half day today. The teachers are marking our report cards." "I see. If you have good reports, you can go to the motion pictures Saturday."

Hearing that, both boys stopped bothering Honey and started their homework at the kitchen table.

Sam turned to Anna. "Sit down, dear. I've good news. While in Masontown, I learned that the Yankovics might be moving to Pittsburgh. If they do, they'll sell their house on South Main Street. I'd like you to go with me soon to look at the property. It should be easy to convert the front of the house to a store." He paused. "There's another matter. I learned that there's no Syrian Orthodox Church in Masontown. So I talked with several of the Syrian businessmen about starting a church in Brownsville."

Anna wiped her hands on her apron and sat down beside the boys. She pulled her hair into a tighter bun, as she always did while cooking. "Why Brownsville?" she asked.

"The land there is cheap compared to Masontown. Four of us agreed to purchase a piece of land on Spring Street where we can build a small church."

"Samuel, can we afford a house *and* contribute to a new church? Then there's Mitelj and Martha. My parents are getting older. Only God knows how long they'll be able to care for my babies—and they're not babies anymore at thirteen and eleven."

"We've talked about this many times. I thought we agreed that they'd join our family after we open the store. With the town's help and with the other businessmen, it won't take much of our savings to start a little church."

Before Anna could reply, John asked, "*Abb*, I've been hearing you and *Umm* talk about my other sister and brother. Please, can they come over? We'll be nice to them. Won't we, Tony?"

Tony just grinned.

"They'll be with our family soon enough," Sam told his sons. "Your mother and I agreed to wait until we have our own store."

Anna shook her head slowly in agreement and turned back to her cooking as she blessed herself. *There's no point in arguing with Samuel about the timing or money. Bless his heart, he's good at saving and prudent when it comes to buying. Yet at times like this, I wonder. St. Gerald, pray for us.*

One week later Sam found out that the Yankovic house was indeed for sale. While the older boys were in school, Elena watched the younger children and Anna went to visit the property with Sam. They parked in front of the yellow brick home and walked around to the back first.

"Look at the rich vines on the arbor, with the benches and yard beneath," Anna pointed out. "What an idyllic place to read to the children and for the girls to play. And the back alley—it must lead to somewhere."

"Yes, Anna. Most alleys do." Sam grinned.

"Stop teasing me."

"If you turn right into the alley and walk down two blocks, you can cross the street to Masontown High School. And the Catholic Church is at the corner. We're in a good location for a home and a store."

"But it's right on Main Street. Not much space for the boys to play and run. They have so much energy, those sons of ours."

"They'll get plenty of that in school and on weekends. Summers, I'll have them busy helping in the store."

Mr. and Mrs. Yankovic welcomed them in to look through the house. There was a large front living room with a kitchen behind it and a small reading room off that. A door at the back of the kitchen led to the arbor and patio.

"Why, Sam, look at this kitchen," Anna said. "Just what we need for our growing family. The oven looks new, and there's room for a large table with many chairs."

"Let's see the rest of the house." When they were in the garage, Sam said, "Big enough for three automobiles—and a large area if we want to add another oven for baking."

"Dear, are you thinking of another automobile?"

"No. But John and Tony will someday. Besides, I can work on ours in a garage this size."

There were steps between the kitchen and front living room leading down to the garage, and another set leading to the second floor. After seeing the garage and the four bedrooms and bath upstairs, they thanked the owners. "Can we get back in touch with you by Saturday?" Sam said. "My wife and I are interested in purchasing your house. I'll need to check details with my bank. When are you looking to finalize the sale?"

"Take your time," Mr. Yankovic told Sam. "We'll talk again Saturday. If I can sell to you, I'll be pleased, since your reputation is excellent."

As the men shook hands, Anna looked at Sam with admiration. *He gets more handsome every day. So honorable and smart.*

On the drive home, she talked about decorating the house and remodeling the front room to become the store. "You know, I think John would help you with converting the front entrance to a store window—and Anthony too."

"Yes, John certainly can help me build the shelves and cabinets for displays. We can start after the purchase and continue to work on the remodel while we live in the house. Our John and Tony can help."

"That may keep those two out of trouble. They can be rowdy."

"Anna, they're just boys. When they want to, they can be good—also, helpful with the younger ones. And I'm thankful they're doing well in school."

"Well, Sam, I suppose you're right."

LINDA HANNA LLOYD

Back in New Salem, Sam went to the store to talk with Anthony about the purchase and his decision to move.

Anthony sighed. "I know you're ready to open your own store, Sam. You've been working very hard for your dream. But I'll miss you and your family. All of New Salem will."

Later that evening, Sam, along with Anna, talked with the children about the move.

"Dad, how far is Masontown? Will I be able to visit my friends here?" asked John.

Sam pulled out his map. "You see, we're here, and Masontown is southwest about twenty-five miles. Over here is Uniontown, about thirty miles. We aren't too far."

"Is Masontown bigger than New Salem?"

"Son, there are about 1,500 people living there. It's definitely larger than our town."

"But where will we go to school?"

"Masontown Elementary, and later the high school. They're close to our new home. You and Tony can easily walk to school."

Tony chimed in, "Can I go with you to help build the store?"

"I'm planning to take you and John next Saturday or Sunday so you can see our new house and where the store will be."

Mary exclaimed, "I want to go! John and Tony always get to go with you." "Darling, let your *abb* take the boys, and we'll go another time," Anna said.

"Mary, you and I will make a special time to go together," Sam said as he patted her head.

That evening, after the children were asleep, Anna approached Sam. "May we talk?"

"Certainly. Let's sit in the living room. We seldom have time alone anymore."

Anna took off her apron and took her hair out of the chignon. It fell to her shoulders in curly waves. She looked as young as she did at eighteen.

"This is all happening fast—the move, the store, and the church. Do you understand how much I miss my other children?" Her cheeks glistened with sadness. Tiny tears, like raindrops, rolled down her cheeks.

"Anna, my dear, I thought I did. But you know how important the store is to me. Didn't we agree?"

"But then, why the church too? We could use that money to bring them over."

"Anna, there are many other families giving money for the church. The building is going up quickly, and we should be able to open the church in early summer." He moved over on the sofa, closer to her.

She leaned her head on his chest and mumbled through her tears, "You're right. I've been feeling melancholy lately. I'm fearful Martha and Mitelj may stop remembering me."

"You're their mother. They won't forget you. You write to them and to your parents often. Darling, they're thirteen and eleven, and that may sound old. But they're too young to travel alone." He rubbed her back. Later he said, "Let's go to bed."

Honey's cries woke Anna up early the next morning. As she dressed her youngest, she smiled to herself. *I'm a blessed woman with a husband who loves our four healthy children and me. Today I'm not going to dwell on what the future will bring to me. Inshallah.*

The next week Sam met with officials of the Uniontown Bank, where he had significant savings. When he was back home, he told Anna the news. "The bank has approved the loan for our house."

Anna had her own news. "Oh dear. It may be too soon." "Whatever do you mean?"

"I was at the doctor today. We're having a baby."

Sam smiled. "Anna, it's not too soon. You know I love children, and I want a large family. This is perfect. I hope we have more."

"That's why I was feeling so sad earlier this week. I should know the signs by now." She half-smiled as Sam took her into his arms.

"When can we expect this little one?"

"December. Maybe on your birthday."

In October of 1917, the first service was celebrated in St. Ellien of Homs Syria Orthodox Church. Sam and Anna took all the children.

As they walked up to the entrance of the church, John stopped to look at the sign. "Ellien? That's my middle name. And it sounds like a girl's name."

"Son, it's a boy's. You were named after St. Ellien, who lived in Homs Syria," Sam explained.

"What did he do to become a saint?"

"He studied and practiced medicine. When he treated people, he didn't accept money for his cures." Sam gave his son a gentle nudge. "Let's go into the church now. The service is about to begin."

During the coffee hour afterward, they mingled and admired the church interior. At the bottom of one of the stained-glass windows, there was this inscription: *Donated by Sam Hanna Family.*

27

Shortly after the church dedication, Sam began to remodel the storefront. It wasn't long before word spread, and several other men came to help him. John and Anthony were there when they could get away from their own businesses. The men started by taking out the two walls in the front, one at a time, and replacing them with glass windows. They left the front door to be between the windows. Once that was finished, the interior would be easy.

While remodeling, Sam continued to work at Abraham's. Anna busied herself getting ready for the move. Still active in the Ladies Society, she worked with Sadie and Elena to train the new volunteers. She knew that after she moved away, the group would need more help.

By the end of November, the storefront was completed. But there was still work to do inside—installing shelves, countertops, and glass cases. John and Anthony were in school when Sam and Anna took Mary and Honey to see the building project. As they walked through the room that would be the store, Anna paused to lean against the wall.

"Anna, are you feeling sick?" Sam asked.

"No, just tired. What would you think about waiting until the summer to move?"

"That would be wise. I don't want you doing too much work. We should move at the end of this school year. It'll be easier for the boys and for you."

Just then, Mary tugged on her mother's skirt, saying, "Show me my bedroom."

After Sam and Anna took the girls through the house, all four of them walked down Main Street to talk with the merchants. Sam bought the girls a treat in Vignola's Drugstore, then they drove home to New Salem.

Sam was able to establish customers by peddling while getting the store completed. He purchased inventory from Anthony. For the most part, the people around Masontown had gone to Uniontown to shop, so they were happy to have Sam delivering their purchases to their homes and businesses

Many of his customers lived in rural areas and welcomed his visits. On Saturdays, Sam worked with Anthony.

Anna gave birth to Louis Franklin on December 17, 1917: 'Louis' after— well, no one understood until Anna explained that it was her father's name. 'Franklin' was inspired by Sam's admiration for Franklin D. Roosevelt, Assistant Secretary of the Navy. Louis's brothers and sisters called him 'Louie.' The girls wouldn't leave him alone. They told all their friends they'd been given a new baby for Christmas. Anna taught Mary how to change a diaper. When Anna rocked the baby, all Honey wanted to do was to sit on her mother's lap too.

Louie's brothers were happy to have more independence. When Sam had time, he took them to Masontown to work with him on the store. While Tony handed him nails, one by one, John learned to pound them into the wall for the shelving. By June, they'd made progress. Sam estimated that the store would be ready to open in the fall.

That summer, when it came time to pack and move, the family had help from many friends in New Salem. Anna had a difficult time saying goodbye to Sadie, Elena, and Mary Benko. She was comforted when Mary reminded her that Masontown wasn't that far away.

The day after the move, Anna was in her new kitchen when she heard a knock on the back door.

"What a surprise to see you so soon!" she exclaimed when John and Elena walked in.

"We want to help you unpack," John said.

"And we brought dinner." Elena set a basket down on the table, which was already covered with dishes and stacked pots and pans. She looked around. "This kitchen is so big, and there's so much storage. Just tell me where to put things."

"You're such dear friends." Then she called, "Sam, come see who's here."

"You're not working, John?" Sam asked, walking into the kitchen.

John smiled. "I have the time to help you. And a summer day off is good for me. Where shall we begin?"

Sam motioned toward the chairs. "First, sit for *ahweh*. Later we can start in the front room."

The Store

The first Saturday in November, Hanna's Department Store had its grand opening day, with the children dressed in their finest. John was nine years old, Anthony, seven, Mary, five, and Honey, three. They were excited to get to help. Sam thought back to the opening of Abraham's Dry Goods, and he couldn't help but smile to himself. Just like Tony Abraham, his children loved to climb up on the rolling ladder.

The storefront faced South Main Street. Mounted outside it was the American flag. The cash register was at the front counter, facing out to the entrance. On both sides of the register were counters stocked with patterns, thread, undergarments, and socks. The watches and jewelry were displayed in glass cases. The shelves from floor to ceiling displayed fabric, work boots, and shoes for women, men, and children.

At the rear of the store, just before the entrance to the door that led to the kitchen of the house, Anna kept a table stocked all that day with coffee and *baklava* ready for customers. She enjoyed talking to them as they browsed. Mary tried to keep an eye on Louie—who often had his fun crawling under the table and pulling on the tablecloth.

At the end of opening day, Sam and Anna, exhausted and brimming with excitement, sat down with the family for dinner.

"Children, thank you for your help today," Sam told them. "Would you like a special job *every* day? When it's time to close the store?"

"Yes," they replied, some louder than others.

"You each think what that job would be, and tomorrow we can talk more about this. You'll be expected to complete your homework either before or after dinner. If we find that you don't, you won't be allowed to help in the store." They soon came to their father with their ideas. John and Tony would count the cash. Mary would sweep and straighten the shelves. Honey said she wanted to help her mother change the front window display.

The store quickly became a family effort.

28

Sam had finally purchased and sent tickets for Martha and Mitelj to move to America. She was fourteen years old, and he was sixteen. The ship was to arrive on January 22, 1921.

Finally, the day came—cold and blustery—and Sam, John, and Tony boarded the train to New York.

"Dad, are we going to see where your ship came in from Syria?" Tony asked on the way.

"Yes, we are. That was so long ago."

"How long?" asked John.

"Sixteen years. I was only seventeen. When we get home, remind me to show you my journal. . . . Before we meet your brother and sister, we're going to spend time with a friend of mine in the city."

They took the trolley to George Nader's shop. The wide-eyed boys quietly watched Sam order goods for the store. Then John spotted the cast iron toy cars. "Dad, look at these cars. Will you buy some to sell in the store?"

Tony added, "Please. Our friends will like them."

"We can try a few to see how they sell. You boys pick out a dozen, and then you can each pick out one to be your own." Sam watched his sons carefully chose the items. They took their time, as if buying their first real automobiles.

Soon they were off to take the ferry to Ellis Island. Sam wanted to get there early just in case there were any problems with the children during registration. He had telegraphed Anna's parents to let them know he'd be there in time for the ship's arrival. By now, Sam knew how to navigate the immigration system. He held up his handmade sign with Martha's and Mitelj's names on it.

John and Tony looked carefully at the passengers in the Great Hall. Finally they spotted a boy and girl who resembled the ones they'd seen in photos.

A disappointed Martha had tears running down her cheeks when she saw that her mother wasn't with the strangers who had come to meet her and her brother.

Sam walked up to them. "Mitelj and Martha, I'm Sam, your stepfather. These are your half-brothers, John and Tony."

"Where's our mother?" asked Mitelj.

"I'm sorry," Sam said. "Your mother is about to have a baby and couldn't make this trip. You'll see her soon. For now, you have to go upstairs for your physicals. John and Tony and I will go with you."

Even though Martha was crying, she passed all the exams. But her brother failed the eye exam. This made Martha cry even more.

Mitelj was prepared in case this happened: He knew they could go on to relatives in Brazil. "Martha, we can stay here in the holding area until tomorrow and board a steamship to Rio de Janeiro," he told his sister. "That is what I have to do. Would you like to go with me?"

"No, Mitelj. I'm sorry, but I want to see our mother. It's been too many years."

Sam agreed with the plan and made sure that Mitelj had enough money to make the additional trip. After handing the boy the cash, he said, "Please send us a telegram when you arrive in Brazil. And try to come back for a visit when possible. Good luck, and may God be with you."

John and Tony watched all of this, not knowing what to say.

So for the third time Sam made the trip from Ellis Island to Penn Station, then to New York City, and on to Uniontown, Pennsylvania. This time, the train from Penn Station would go directly to the station in Uniontown.

Martha struggled on the trip to her new home. John and Tony tried to talk to her, but she sobbed most of the time. Halfway there, John was able to humor her into talking about France and her life in Syria. Then she became interested in what life in America was like for the boys. Sam was pleased to see that Martha had calmed down, but he remained worried. As the train approached Uniontown, he pointed out the sights to her, praying silently that she would come to love her new family.

When they'd left the station, the boys pointed to their auto in the parking "Dad, it's still here," said Tony.

"Son, I'm not surprised. I locked it up tight. Now, children, hop in and let's drive home."

Anna was peering out the window when the automobile turned into the back driveway. She ran out to greet her newly arrived children. "There you are, my dear. How beautiful." Anna hugged Martha as if no time had passed.

"How could you leave me for so many years?" These were the first words to come from Martha's mouth. "Don't you love me?"

"Ah, yes. I prayed for you and Mitelj every day. But the time wasn't right. Surely you must understand the cost and difficulty of sending young children alone on a passenger ship to America."

"I've tried. But I cried for you every night."

"Here you are now with me. You weren't old enough to know it, but when your father died I had no choice but to make a better life for myself in America. And I couldn't travel with you and Mitelj as babies. Please forgive me. I love Sam, and I hope you'll grow to love him and our children."

Martha looked intensely at her mother. "I'll try."

Anna glanced around, then at Sam. She could see the worry in his eyes. "But where is Mitelj?"

Martha told her mother the story, with Sam interjecting comments. "Well, at least he'll be with family," Anna said, resigned. "And eventually we'll go visit him."

"I asked Mitelj to send us a telegram when he arrived in Rio de Janeiro. And I gave him money for the trip," said Sam.

Anna hugged him especially hard. "Thank you, dear."

Left to Right: Martha, Tony, Anna (holding
Michael), Honey, Sam (holding Lou), Mary, John
Hanna Family - 1921

Martha found herself among several young siblings, who she soon began mothering while enrolled in Masontown High School. She was a good student and kept her grades up with John and Tony. Both boys were excellent athletes and star football players.

Sam and Anna completed their family with the birth of Michael David in 1921 and of George Peter in 1924. With the new little ones, Martha helped more in the store while Anna was busy with the babies.

Their home was full of life and had plenty of room for the children. There was a large table to seat at least ten in the kitchen. The living room off the kitchen was a family gathering place in the evening. In it was a bookcase filled to overflowing. The children shared bedrooms and didn't seem to mind.

THE SYRIAN PEDDLER

In the basement, Anna had a freezer and an extra oven. She baked endless loaves of Syrian bread, *kibbeh* to freeze. She still loved to sew. In her spare moments, she made curtains for all the windows. Mary showed an interest in helping, and Honey tried. Martha became an expert seamstress and made dresses for the girls.

It wasn't long before the younger boys became a handful. As soon as they could walk down the basement steps, they would open the freezer to take out another loaf of bread—even though they had it at every meal, including breakfast.

"Those boys of ours keep getting into the freezer. For bread," Anna told Sam one day. "Whatever will we do?"

He calmly answered, "Boys will be boys. I'll talk to them when the store closes."

"And then Martha caught them running across the roofs today."

Louie was in the habit of putting on a black cape, calling himself the Riddle Rider, and running across the rooftops, with Michael and George chasing him. He would tease George and call him "Duck," since he ran like the animal. That nickname stuck with George for years.

One evening after such an escapade, Sam called a family meeting. The eight children gathered around the table, trying to avoid their parents' stern faces. By this time, the older children were young adults.

"Louie, I know you're only ten," Sam began. "And Michael, you're only six. And George, you're just four. You're all still young. Even so, you must learn to listen to your mother and Martha. Please try to behave like your older brothers. You *cannot* take out bread anytime you want. If you continue, we'll put a lock on the freezer. And as far as the roof running goes, you know that's dangerous. It must stop immediately."

John spoke up. "Dad, remember what Tony and I were like at their age?"

"I do. But your mother and I didn't have seven children then."

Anna smiled. "We do have good news. John has been accepted to American University in Washington, D.C. And Martha is going to be married to Ralph Ayoub. He's a very nice man from Ohio."

While this discussion was going on, George was secretly playing with his dog, Stubby, that was under the table. There was a loud bark.

Sam looked at his youngest son sternly. "George, we told you Stubby wasn't allowed there."

"Sorry. But no one pays attention to our dog but me." George turned to John. "I'm going to miss you. When will you be back?"

"For sure at Christmas."

Later that same evening, Sam and Anna shared their thoughts over glasses of *arak* as they often did.

"I'm disappointed that John isn't interested in working as a mechanic," Sam said. "He's good with cars—seems to have a sixth sense with repairs."

"Sam, you surprise me. We've talked about the value of a college education. I hope all our boys do the same as John."

"We both know Tony won't. He loves working in the store. And he has a knack with our customers. I'd really like one of our sons to work with me in retail."

"I agree. And it should be Tony. Martha also has a good way of relating to people. I've talked to her about opening a dress shop of her own."

"She's a hard worker. And she's been such a help with the younger ones. Also in the store."

"Thankfully, we've arranged a good match for her. She'll be happy."

Sam rubbed his chin thoughtfully. "I pray she will."

By 1930, Hanna's Department Store was thriving. It could be spotted from a distance by its red awning. The Klondike coal region was booming, while the addition of streetcars running from Lambert, Palmer, and Ronco brought more customers to town

Anna was active in the community and the church—this time with a new Ladies Guild that had the same mission as the ladies group at St. George's. Sam continued to help his customers, and the store became a place to share happy and sad times. During the Great Depression he would allow them to keep a running tab, and from time to time he would say, *God will pay*.

As the younger children grew older, he expected hard work and good grades, and he was firm about the younger boys going to college and serving their country in times of war. Mary and Honey had desires to continue their education after high school, but Sam believed that a woman belonged in the home. He and Anna had hopes that all the children would marry a Greek Orthodox Syrian. Yet they realized and accepted the fact that their sons and daughters were more American than Syrian.

When the children became young adults, serving their country, finishing college, or building a business, Sam became more accepting of their choices.

He took every opportunity to brag about their accomplishments. When he did this, Anna looked at him with admiration and love in her eyes.

Left to Right - Back Row: John, Mary, Tony, Lou
Front Row: Michael, Anna, Sam, George, Honey
Hanna Family - 1930

EPILOGUE

Martha was happy in her marriage to Ralph Ayoub, who was also from Syria. They lived in Yorkville, Ohio, where they raised three daughters. Her love of sewing and retail continued, and she opened a dress shop. In 1946, Sam purchased tickets so that Martha and Anna could visit Mitelj in Rio de Janeiro. Before that time, the only contact they had with him was by mail.

After college, John entered the civil service. He was assigned to a position in Japan, where he supervised all civil service personnel during World War

There, he met Evelyn Dwyer, who worked for the American Red Cross. They married, adopted a baby girl, and shortly after that had a son. Evelyn was pregnant with another child when John was given orders to go to Paris. They decided to turn it down and move back to the United States when their second son and daughter were born.

John started Hanna's Insurance Company in the building next to the department store in Masontown. For a time John and his family lived in Masontown, then eventually moved to Uniontown. John, like his father, had a knack with customers. And if they couldn't make their payments, he always found a way to help them.

Tony became his father's partner in the store. He married Mary Nader. Mary's family was Syrian and owned a retail store in New Castle, Pennsylvania. Mary helped Sam and Tony run the store. Tony and Mary lived in Sam and Anna's house, where they raised four daughters. Tony, like Sam, was involved in the community. He served two terms as the town's mayor. After Tony died, his wife Mary continued to run the store until it closed in 1997.

Mary entered the Women's Army Corp, known as the WAC, during World War II. After training, she served in Manila. She loved the WAC, and it became her career. At the end of the war, she transferred to Albuquerque, New Mexico, where she married and had one son. She and her son, young Sam, went home to visit several times, and eventually they settled in Texas.

THE SYRIAN PEDDLER

Honey married an Irish man, Bill Boyle. Bill worked in construction, while Honey had a beauty salon in their home. She and Bill lived right down the street from Sam's store. Later she went to floral design school and opened a florist shop in Masontown. The last stop in her career was a city government position in Uniontown. Bill and Honey never had children. Honey mothered all her nieces and nephews and hosted many holiday dinners at her home. When Honey passed away, the Hanna cousins enjoyed sharing their fond memories of Aunt Honey.

Louis went to Slippery Rock State College, where he was co-captain of the football team. After he graduated in 1940, he went into the service as an aviation cadet. Then, after eight months of training, he received an honorable discharge when a spot on his eye was detected. Lou was coaching high school football in Cresson, Pennsylvania, when he fell in love with a young Irishwoman named Helen Kimlin, who everyone called Kim. He went home to tell his family, and when he mentioned Helen's parents, Emma and Jack, Sam had a strange look on his face. He wasn't happy about Lou marrying an Irish Catholic, especially after Honey had done the same. Kim and Lou had five children—three daughters and two sons. Lou built a name for himself throughout Corry, Pennsylvania as an outstanding coach and founder of the first football camp for boys in the country. Later he was inducted into the Pennsylvania Hall of Fame. He was active in the community, including serving on the city council.

Michael graduated in 1941 from the University of Pennsylvania. He attended college on a football scholarship and was quarterback and co-captain of the football team. He then went into the U.S. Army. On D-Day, he landed on the beaches of Normandy and later fought his way through France, where he was injured. His deeds gained him a Purple Heart. He came home to Masontown after the war and started an accounting business. When he was looking for a secretary, a friend told him that Katherine Plesh had just moved back to Masontown after working as a riveter in Detroit during the war. He not only hired Katherine, who was Catholic, but also married her. They had four children—two daughters and two sons. At some point, Michael moved his business to Pittsburgh, where he continued a successful accounting and insurance practice.

George served in the U.S. Army during World War II as a Technician Fourth Grade before entering Slippery Rock State College. He transferred to Pennsylvania State University and then went on to West Virginia University for his Master's degree. He began his career as a single man, teaching and coaching close to Masontown. One day Sam took George to visit his friends, Slayman and Magida Abraham, in New Castle, Pennsylvania. Slayman and Magida had five daughters. The oldest, Rose, fell in love with George and he with her. It was a great match for the time: He was handsome, educated, and had a good job, while Rose was beautiful and a great cook. They were married several months later. Finally, Sam had another Syrian daughter-in-law. George and Rose moved to Pittsburgh, where he was a high school principal until he moved to Columbus, Ohio, for a position at Ohio State University. They had two daughters and two sons.

Left to Right - Back Row: Tony, George, John, Lou
Front Row: Michael, Mary, Sam, Honey
Hanna Family - 1958

Anna died in 1947 from complications of appendicitis. She was fifty-nine years old. Sam lived until 1958, dying from a heart attack at the age of seventy-one

Anna and Sam would be dismayed to hear of the bitter conflict and resulting destruction that began in their home country in 2011 and was still unresolved as of January 2017. What they would be happy to hear is that a celebration of the 100th anniversary of St. Ellien Syrian Orthodox Church in Brownsville, Pennsylvania, was planned for October 2017.

ACKNOWLEDGEMENTS

I want to thank the following people, without whom this book would not have been possible.

Mary Hanna Reuter, Shawn Samuel Hanna, Dennis Hanna, Sam Hanna, Nancy Long Hanna, Father Kevin Gregory Long, Laurice Hanna Dailey, Gerri Hanna, Honey Ayoub Gaudio, and Barbara Ayoub Chincheck: For your reviews and background information, as well as the many times you answered my questions and cheered me on.

Rebecca Hanna Ryan: For your very helpful opinions and concrete suggestions, as well as your invaluable encouragement.

Deacon Glenn McIntyre and Susan Solomon: For information about St. Ellien Syria Orthodox Church, Brownsville, Pennsylvania.

Wilbur McIntosh, McIntosh Photography: For your wonderful photos of St. Ellien Church that grace the book cover.

My daughter, Karlyn Johnston Heide: For designing the book cover with such dedication and expertise.

My son and his partner, Derek Johnston and Pat Carney: For providing me work space during my visits and for reviewing my manuscript, until their dog, Tomas, began to snack on the paper. It's true dogs do eat your homework.

Shana Johnson: For your incredible support during the writing courses.

My friends from many walks of life—Mary Comfort, Camille Anthony, Bobbie Dill, Connie Earle, Peggy Sanin, Becky Zeligman, Barbara Latvanas, Marcia Adler, Lisa Thornburg, Mary Kay Cascario, Maher Alzain, Glarih Yazdi Morgan, Gloria Morgan, Cathie and Ron Hanovice: For your unique forms of support and critical review of the manuscript, each of which helped me in different ways.

Rea Keech, author of A Hundred Veils: For your advice during the course of writing and throughout the publishing process.

Elaine DeFrank, ALAS at the Coal and Coke Heritage Center located on the Eberly Campus Penn State Fayette County: For your time to discuss the history of the early 1900's coal mining era in southwestern Pennsylvania, as well as your book recommendations, which were invaluable resources.

Susan Luton: For your editorial expertise, tireless effort, and patience. You were a delight to work with through the many discussions and revisions that resulted in the final manuscript.

Jenny Chandler, Senior Publishing Consultant with Createspace: For your guidance during the interior design process and final publication of the book.

Douglas Seward Lloyd: For being my forever cheerleader. Your daily support and respect for my time was amazing. Now for the champagne.

RESOURCES

Another Time Another World by John A. Enman
Becoming American: The Early Arab Immigrant Experience by Alixa Naff
Between Arab and White by Sarah M. A. Gualtieri
Common Lives of Common Strength by Evelyn A. Hovanec
Crossing the Waters edited by Eric J. Hooglund
Daily Life in Immigrant America 1870–1920 by June Granatir Alexander
Gangs and Outlaws of Western Pennsylvania by Thomas White and Michael Hassett
Strangers in the West by Linda K. Jacobs
Facebook page: You Might Be from Masontown If You Remember Masontown Historical Society

THE SYRIAN PEDDLER
DISCUSSION GUIDE

How would you describe Saddo's feelings as his steamship docked in the New York Harbor? What was the reason Syrians were immigrating to America in the early 1900's?

What was your first impression of Saddo? Do you think his characteristics changed as his name did...He was Saddo, then Samuel, and finally Sam.

How would you describe his most endearing qualities?

In what way does Saddo's job on the S.S. Neustria influence his attitudes?

Emma and Saddo grew to be friends and confidantes; could they have overcome the cultural differences and wed?

What is it about Sam's letters that connect the story?

Did you want Sam to tell Zawhea about his relationship with Emma? If so, why?

Samuel assimilates quickly to life in southwestern Pennsylvania what/who helped him adjust?

Little Tony and Sam have a special relationship. What did you learn about Sam through their friendship?

Mary Benko had eleven children and a farm to care for yet she welcomed Sam and Anna into her home. In what ways was she helpful to them, Did you view her in a mothering role?

How does Sam show his desire to achieve success?

Early on, Sam said' "If you can't pay me, God will." How do you interpret this phrase?
How does the robbery influence Sam's business decisions? Could he have handled his anger differently?

How would you best describe life in New Salem? Do you think Sam would have been as content there if he had not become close to John Nazzif? In what ways does John help Sam?

In what way did leaving her babies in Syria affect Zawhea? How could she have convinced Sam to bring them over sooner? Did Martha ever forgive her mother for leaving her?

What changes did you observe in Sam and Anna as they matured in their marriage? What qualities do they each have to balance their business and family

Could Sam and Anna do more to encourage their daughters as opposed to their sons? In what ways?

As the story ends, were you left wanting to know more about Emma, Anna, and Amina?

ABOUT THE AUTHOR

This is Linda Hanna Lloyd's first novel. She received two creative writing awards from the Institute of Creative Research for her poetry. Linda produced and hosted the Howard Community College Cable Television Health Promotion Series, nine of which won national awards. Linda currently resides in Austin, TX with her husband, where they enjoy walking their newly-adopted puppy, Fidela.

Made in the USA
Lexington, KY
15 January 2019